To her right, she saw him again— or at least his silhouette in the mist.

He walked toward her, growing closer. Staring at the ground, he appeared lost in thought. Probably didn't want to stumble. He didn't know the path like she did.

But there was something about him.

The way he walked, his build…

At that moment, the fog thinned considerably to reveal his face. Sela gasped. Of course, he wasn't David. She'd allowed her longing to get the best of her. But with his dark hair and olive complexion, his trim, athletic build, she saw now why her first thoughts were of David.

Sela remained where she stood, watching him move toward her, waiting to see his reaction. The stranger took one last step, then his troubled gaze drew up.

When his eyes met hers, eerie familiarity rolled through her. Again, she thought there was something about him, but she didn't know what.

ELIZABETH GODDARD

is a seventh-generation Texan who recently spent five years in beautiful southern Oregon, which serves as a setting for some of her novels. She is now back in East Texas, living near her family. When she's not writing, she's busy homeschooling her four children. Beth is the author of several novels and novellas. She's actively involved in several writing organizations including American Christian Fiction Writers (ACFW) and loves to mentor new writers.

Books by Elizabeth Goddard

HEARTSONG PRESENTS

HP777—*Seasons of Love*
HP893—*Disarming Andi*
HP913—*Exposing Amber*
HP933—*Praying for Rayne*
HP978—*Under the Redwood Tree*
HP993—*Sheltering Love*

Hearts in the Mist

Elizabeth Goddard

Heartsong Presents

To Dan—thank you for always believing in me.

A note from the Author:

I love to hear from my readers! You may correspond with me by writing:

Elizabeth Goddard
Author Relations
P.O. Box 9048
Buffalo, NY 14240-9048

ISBN-13: 978-0-373-48628-1

HEARTS IN THE MIST

This edition issued by special arrangement with Barbour Publishing, Inc., 1810 Barbour Drive, Uhrichsville, Ohio, U.S.A.

Chapter 1

"Befriend her. Charm her. Whatever it takes."

Whatever it takes?

Evan Black bristled at the words, but he didn't respond. Through the panoramic window of his father's large corner office at Blackwood Development, Evan watched waves crash against the rocky outcropping below. The coast was beautiful here—maybe that's why his father had opened a regional office in Crescent City, California.

"Three hundred acres of prime real estate. That's all that's left before we can move forward." Robert Black's tone let Evan know he wanted his son's attention.

Turning slowly, Evan peered into his father's dark eyes. Working for his father's development company hadn't been easy, considering the elder Black didn't believe in showing any favoritism to his own son.

Evan had started at the bottom as a carpenter because his father wanted him to have hands-on experience from the ground up, working in every facet in the real estate management and development industry in a company that had designed and constructed everything from hotels and single-family homes to hydroelectric projects.

And now he'd assigned Evan this housing development, bringing him from the Blackwood home office, and his home, in Virginia Beach. Completing this project to satisfaction would land him on his father's handpicked management team as vice president of construction.

He'd worked harder than anyone else, and now his father dangled the key to success. The slight smile on his father's lips hinted that he was satisfied he had Evan's attention.

"Just picture it, Evan. A private, gated housing community and resort in the middle of the majestic redwoods, a vast panorama of natural beauty, and a forty-acre golf course created by one of the top designers."

"Sounds like you have it all figured out. Why'd you need me on this project again?" Evan forced some humor into his tone. This move might end up being more permanent than temporary. Evan wasn't sure he wanted to leave Virginia Beach. Then again, getting some face time with his father might mend a wound that never seemed to heal.

"I don't have it all figured out; I'm just showing you how I envision things. Then there's that three hundred acres of prime real estate," he repeated, dragging out the last words as he pushed a pin into a map on the wall. The Smith River wove through the redwoods around the pin and then spilled into the Pacific. "Get her to sell her land. The project is at a standstill until all the pieces are in place."

"And once I've completed this housing development, and you're satisfied, then you'll make me a vice president on your management team." Which only included three other people, and they weren't related to Robert Black.

"The prize is within your reach, son." His father smiled broadly and clapped Evan on the shoulder, an unusual gesture for him.

But Evan's gut burned at the tactics his father had suggested. The founder of Blackwood Development had spent years jumping through the California property hoops to gain the surrounding acreage for development. Why did he need three hundred more? "What's so important about her land that we can't move forward if she won't sell?"

The man's smile dropped. He made his way around his mahogany executive desk to ease into the high-backed, maroon leather chair, clasping his hands across his trim midsection. Evan favored his father and imagined that's what he'd look like in another thirty years. The man allowed only a little gray to show at the temples of his thick dark hair. Lean muscle sculpted his physique from his early years spent in construction. Now he played tennis to keep in shape and always sported a tan on top of his slightly olive complexion.

His father peered at him. Evan never liked it when his father looked at him that way. He would have thought by now, at thirty-two, he wouldn't shrink under his father's glower. He'd tolerated the man's harsh behavior this long; just a little longer and he could achieve the success he'd worked for all these years. The success he wanted. His father had started and built the company from the ground up and had seen the fruit of his efforts. Evan was more than ready to step into the position he'd worked and been groomed for.

But more important, he was ready to see the glimmer of approval in his father's eyes. To hear his father say he was proud of him. And yet…he had the uncanny sense that even *that* wouldn't vanquish the emptiness inside.

"What's so important about it?" Mocking him, his father repeated the question.

Asking it in the first place had made Evan appear weak-minded. Unfit for an executive-level position at the company. Unfit to be Robert Black's son. But there was something else about his father's request that left Evan uneasy. Something he wasn't being told.

"I get that the Smith River runs through the property, and including that in our plans would increase the value exponentially, but what *aren't* you telling me?"

He held steady under his father's hard gaze. "You're shrewd, Evan. That's why you're the man for this task."

Evan's father had evaded the question, but Evan hadn't thought getting the answer would be easy. He'd let it drop.

For now.

"If you've already approached this woman about the property, how do you expect me to have success where you failed?" *Careful with your choice of words, Evan.*

"I didn't say that I personally approached her—that's why I have employees. People to do the dirty work. But their efforts have failed." His father paused as if considering his next words carefully. "But as far as you having success in this situation, you sell yourself short, son. If you're going to be a part of this decision-making team, part of management, then realize your power. You're young and virile. There's never a time I've been with you that women weren't looking your way." Again his father paused. He ran his hand over the smooth wood grain of his desk. "Sela Fox is a widow. All you have to do is show up. My guess is that she'll do the talking. Maybe even the wooing."

Are you out of your mind? Evan made to protest—but his father held up a hand, silencing him. Evan ground his teeth.

"She's young and beautiful. You won't find it distasteful to spend time in her company."

Bile rose in Evan's throat. How could his father ask him

to do such a thing? Had he forgotten that Evan had been through a hard breakup two years ago? Now his father was asking him to toy with a woman's heart? Or allow her to toy with his? Evan wasn't that kind of man. That his father could think he was sickened him.

No. His father had crossed a line this time. Evan formulated his words—they could be the last he ever spoke to his father as an employee of Blackwood Development.

The elder Black stood, jamming his hands in his pockets, and strolled to the large window. He gazed through the glass at the Pacific. Behind him, Evan watched as storm clouds broiled dark and hostile in the west.

"I know you think I've been tough on you. But it was for your own good. I had to work hard to get where I am today. That builds character and makes you strong. Though I can see you're struggling with my request, you have no idea how important it is." His father angled his head toward Evan. "I look forward to the day when you and I can work together side by side to grow this company. To branch out to other things."

Evan's tongue grew thick in a dry, parched mouth. Was that assurance of a more congenial relationship? Or another empty promise? Time spent together. The validation from his father he longed for even as an adult. It sounded too good to be true.

Robert Black squeezed Evan's shoulder. "Walk the property where it meets ours to see what I'm talking about. Then meet Sela Fox. You don't have to tell her who you are or talk to her about selling. Just meet her first, then tell me your decision. Can you at least do that for me?"

It was the first time that his father actually asked Evan rather than demanded that he do something—though he'd never asked anything like this before. How could Evan refuse at least the first part of his father's request?

All he had to do was meet her and then tell his father he couldn't go through with using manipulative tactics to persuade her into selling her property.

Befriend her. Charm her. Whatever it takes.

Evan sighed. He wasn't a fool. Refusing his father wouldn't be that easy, especially with the position in the company that Evan wanted dangling in the balance.

But he'd find a way…whatever it took.

Fog hung in the air, wrapping Sela Fox in a moist blanket of mist.

She stepped around a sword fern and pressed her hand against the rough bark of a young redwood—still giant in proportion to trees of other species. She couldn't see twenty feet in front of her. The marine fog was thick this morning.

But she knew the path well—she walked these woods every morning before her busy day working at her gift shop for locals and tourists began. Careful to keep the handcrafted guitar she carried from harm, she pressed deeper into the woods across the river from her home.

She found the stump she was looking for and cradled the guitar—David's favorite—as she sat. Positioning the guitar, she strummed the familiar chords that had always brought her comfort. Clumsily at first, then as she closed her eyes and relaxed to the sound, she imagined David playing the instrument.

Sela sighed and dropped her hand to her side. It was no use. She'd never been able to play like him, nor were her guitars the masterpieces he created. But that wasn't what bothered her.

David wasn't here to play.

Something was wrong with her. He'd been gone for five years now, having died in a boating accident. Shouldn't she have moved on by now? But the home she'd shared with him and the property they owned in the redwoods cocooned her in the memories. In the past.

How did she break free? She wasn't sure she even wanted to.

Her high school sweetheart, David, was the only man she'd ever loved. Holding on to the memories and what they had together had been her way of keeping him with her—the only way she knew. But loneliness had set in long ago. She missed his arms around her, the tenderness shared between a husband and wife.

Lord, help me to let him go.

Sela stared ahead, lost in memories. Lost in the fog. Even if she let David go and moved on, she'd still have the loneliness to deal with.

For an instant, the mist thinned a few yards to her right. Someone was there. The fog thickened again, moving in and out like a cloud and hiding whoever it was.

David!

Sela slowly stood. She was losing her mind. Of course it wasn't David. She slid a hand to her throat. Still, there was someone else out there. She'd never feared walking the woods, especially on her own property.

She remained frozen in time like the centuries-old redwood next to her, and waited. The mist shrouded everything, including sound. She heard nothing. Saw only what encircled her for a few feet.

Finally, Sela took a step forward. She continued to walk in the direction she'd seen the man. After a time, the mist began to lift. If someone was out there, and she hadn't just imagined it, what was he doing on her property?

Minutes passed. Time was getting away, and Sela would need to prepare for her day at the shop. Whoever she'd seen had probably stumbled across the property line by accident. She started back.

To her right, she saw him again—or at least his silhouette in the mist. He walked toward her, growing closer. Staring at the ground, he appeared lost in thought. Probably didn't want to stumble. He didn't know the path like she did.

But there was something about him.

The way he walked, his build...

At that moment, the fog thinned considerably to reveal his face. Sela gasped. Of course, he wasn't David. She'd allowed her longing to get the best of her. But with his dark hair and olive complexion, his trim, athletic build, she saw now why her first thoughts were of David.

Sela remained where she stood, watching him move toward her, waiting to see his reaction. The stranger took one last step, then his troubled gaze drew up.

When his eyes met hers, eerie familiarity rolled through her. Again, she thought there was something about him, but she didn't know what.

Surprise and something else—an appreciation that made her blush—registered in his eyes. His frown twitched into a hesitant grin.

Sela smiled. "Nice morning for a walk." What else did one say under the circumstances?

His grin growing, he kept his eyes trained on her. "I'd prefer to see where I'm going."

Sela took a step closer. "That might explain how you stumbled onto my property."

"I'm sorry." He instantly lost his smile. "*Your* property?"

"It was a simple mistake, I'm sure. Do you need help finding your way back?"

The man scratched his thick head of dark hair and

glanced behind him. When he looked back, his smile had returned. "No. I think I'm good. I'm Evan, by the way."

"Nice to meet you, Evan. I'm Sela. I own the burl gift shop across the river, and the surrounding acreage."

"You're fortunate. It's beautiful here."

Sela felt her own smile grow unsteady. *Not as fortunate as you might think.*

Evan's gut soured.

By not giving her full disclosure about who he really was and why he was there, he was already working the situation. On the other hand, in business, negotiations were expected—which meant he wasn't required to give full disclosure at this juncture.

None of that applied here, or at least he wanted none of it to apply, and yet he couldn't bring himself to tell her his whole story—why he was out exploring this morning. What her property had to do with it.

She'd stepped from the mist like an angel, carrying a guitar, no less, and stunned him with her beauty. With one look, she'd unsettled him. Now learning that she was Sela Fox, Evan was more troubled.

When she said nothing more, Evan decided to disengage before he said too much. "Well, I'll just be heading back the way I came. Maybe I'll see you around."

She smiled, wisps of her auburn hair caressing her cheek. Gorgeous.

"Yes. Maybe we'll see each other around." He had the fleeting sense her words were laced with hope.

Evan swallowed and turned his back on her, traipsing back in the direction he'd come from. He'd seen the subtly marked property lines, but with the fog, admittedly, he'd been a little lost and strolled onto her property.

Now that he'd met her, he liked her.

Really liked her.

He wanted to get to know her better, and not for the reasons his father had given. His father knew very well that Evan would be drawn to her. He was probably counting on Evan's loneliness, just like he counted on Sela's, to bring them together.

Evan's mood soured as he stomped through the incredible natural setting soon to be destroyed to make room for more homes. Finally he shoved through a thick mass of ferns and escaped the forest.

His father would want an answer, but Evan hadn't formulated one yet. He almost hated the man for putting him in this position. But a person shouldn't hate his own father, should he?

Chapter 2

At least I won't look like a stalker.

Sela's gift shop was busy today—a surprise considering the secluded location—so Evan wouldn't stand out as he sat in his Tahoe across the road, watching. Wood carvings of all shapes and sizes—much of them of wildlife—were positioned outside the shop in the front and on the side. Redwood burl, he guessed, hence the name, Smith River Redwood Burl Gift Shop.

Surely Sela hadn't carved them, then again, maybe she had.

A young couple browsed the carvings. Evan chuckled to himself, wondering where one would put that type of statue. Front yard? Living room?

He watched and waited, trying to decide what to do. Trying to get up his nerve. He wanted to see her again but was torn. A week had passed since he'd first walked both the property meant for an upscale subdivision and the property his father wanted him to persuade Sela to sell.

He'd avoided women and getting entangled in a romantic relationship since Rachel. But his brief encounter with Sela, her subtle beauty, snagged something inside him.

In that week he'd also dodged facing his father, who'd been traveling, and evaded giving his decision—a decision that Evan had made before meeting Sela.

That's why his father had been confident that Evan wouldn't so easily dismiss spending time with her. He'd said that Evan was shrewd, but Robert Black was the shrewd one.

It disgusted Evan. Now that he'd met her, he definitely couldn't use her like that, if he ever could. His father's request was out of the question.

But couldn't Evan spend time with her, get to know her, without agreeing to his father's plan to convince her to sell her property? Not if he wanted the position his father dangled. Why had he spent what seemed like a lifetime working his way to the top of a company if he could never reach his goal?

A woman exited the gift shop. Evan stiffened when he saw the familiar auburn hair. Sela walked another woman to her car and chatted animatedly then hugged her. From this distance, the woman looked similar to Sela—a sister maybe? Sela waved good-bye as the other woman drove away. He watched Sela walk back inside, a little bounce in her step.

Argh. He *was* a stalker. Evan pressed his head against the seat back. What if he spent time with her because he wanted to see her? They'd become friends for an entirely different reason than his father's scheme, and he could then discuss selling the property without being underhanded. Or maybe he wouldn't discuss it at all.

Yes. That seemed like the right course, all things considered. One thing for certain, Evan couldn't get to know Sela by sitting in his vehicle across the street and watching her from a distance.

He started the ignition and drove from the street into the small parking lot. When he opened the door to the Tahoe, his palms grew moist. What was the matter with him? It wasn't like he hadn't known his share of women, that is, until he'd fallen for Rachel. And his father had been right—women seemed to like Evan right off. But he hated how his father had contrived to exploit that.

Evan slammed the door and strolled toward the shop. He squeezed the door handle and paused, reconsidering his plan. He couldn't see how this would end well, and yet his desire to see her again drove him forward.

What was it about his brief meeting with her? He couldn't know her well enough yet to be this nervous. Evan pulled the door open and stepped inside. The light scent of incense enveloped him. A few customers stood about, looking at knickknacks—both elegant and unsophisticated. Carvings of all kinds and shapes, both beautiful and coarse, drew Evan's attention.

Evan moseyed around the store, waiting for Sela to finish with a customer. He hoped she would see him and approach him first. A couple of burly, lumberjack-looking men entered through the front door and stalked to the counter.

Sela thanked her customer and smiled at the men. "It's just this way," she said and led them through a door in the back.

"Can I help you?"

The question startled Evan. He glanced away from Sela to see an older woman with short gray hair smiling up at him. "Were you looking for something specific?"

He hadn't noticed another employee in the store. Had she seen him watching Sela? "Uh, no. I'm browsing, hoping that something will catch my eye." In truth, everything in the store fascinated him. "But if I could ask a question—where do you get all these carvings?"

Her face brightened. "We provide a place for local artists to display their work. Paintings, pottery, carvings, jewelry, you name it."

"All of these are from local people?"

"Yes sir, most, at least. There are items that Mrs. Fox brings in from outside the area. Initially, only the burl carvings were sold, but the last couple a years she added additional items to attract more tourists and local folks looking for a gift."

Evan nodded, pleased that he'd learned something about Sela already.

"Let me show you something," the woman said then scuttled away, apparently expecting Evan to follow.

She paused before several detailed paintings of the redwoods on the wall. "Mrs. Fox's sister is an up-and-coming artist. She was just in this afternoon."

"Nice. Very nice." Evan smiled. Something had definitely caught his eye. He knew what he would buy. Purchasing her sister's art would surely go a long way in gaining Sela's favor. Evan reminded himself that he wasn't here to work for his father. He simply had an interest in Sela, not her property. "I'll take it."

The woman smiled. Did she work on commission?

"Which one?" she asked.

"All of them."

Her eyes grew wide. "All…but you don't even know how much—"

"You're right." That would be going too far. Evan looked a little closer, and then he saw it—one of the paintings reminded him of the morning he met Sela. "I'll take the larger one with the misty redwoods and the sunbeams."

"A good choice."

Would Sela come back into the store to see him make the purchase? His stomach swirled with nausea. Was he really that conniving? He didn't recall doing anything like this before, even when he'd first met Rachel.

"Will this be all?"

Evan considered his answer, glancing at his watch. He had a few minutes to spare. "No. I'd like to look around some more."

Sela opened the door from the back and held it while the two burly men groaned and strained and turned a huge block of wood this way and that, maneuvering it through the door.

"If you'll excuse me a minute," the salesclerk said, "I need to check out a customer. Take your time." The salesclerk left Evan's side to help another customer at the cash register.

Sela attempted to move display cases, clearly distressed. Evan rushed to her side, next to a shelf that held glass objects. "Let me help," he said.

"Oh, thank you." She glanced up and recognition warmed her eyes. "You, again."

"Yes, me again. I'm not lost today, though." Evan winked, liking the way her eyes had reacted when she saw him. He assisted her in lifting the shelf slowly and carefully. Though a few items fell over, they didn't break.

"We couldn't get the desk out the door in the back, so this was our only choice," she said, her voice strained.

"Don't worry, we'll get it." Evan assisted her in moving a few more shelves, and the burly men lugged the chunk of wood—had she called it a desk?—out the front door as Evan and Sela held the double doors open wide.

The men continued hauling the slab desk with a rustic redwood base into the truck. Evan liked the desk. It was unique. Striking.

"Where are they taking it?" he asked, following Sela out to the truck.

"I'm redecorating—it really isn't a practical desk for me so I never use it. I inherited it along with this shop, I'm afraid. Nor do I have room for it in the store, so it's going to a furniture store in town. The owner has agreed to let me sell it on consignment."

Evan smiled. "I'll take it."

He wasn't buying the desk to garner her favor. He wanted it—for his office when he got his promotion; for his home, until he did.

The thought of the promotion suddenly soured his mood.

Sela stared in silence at the man she'd met just last week when he'd stumbled onto her property. Finally his words sunk in, and she smiled. "Really? Just like that?"

"As soon as I saw the desk, I knew I had to have it."

"That's…wow. Okay, then. Where can these guys deliver it?"

His smile wavered. "Have them take it to the furniture store, but let the owner know I'm on my way over to buy it. I need to make room for it before it gets delivered."

She looked at the furniture movers and nodded. "You heard the man, deliver it as planned."

After the truck pulled away, Sela turned her attention back to the stranger she'd met in the woods. "Evan, is it?"

"You remembered."

"It's not every day a girl runs into a guy lost in the woods." Sela moved back into the shop and began restoring the displays. Evan followed and helped.

"By the way, thank you for helping me," she said. "That could have been a disaster."

"You're welcome." He assisted her in lifting the last display. Then he started putting the glass figurines back in place.

Clara cleared her throat. "Sir, are you still interested in the painting?"

"The painting?" Sela asked.

"Before I saw the desk, I wanted the painting. And I still want it, if that's okay." He offered up a sheepish grin.

"Of course it's okay. Why wouldn't it be?" Sela laughed. "You're a funny guy."

"That's me, the funny guy." He grinned and tilted his head just so. "I admit I might have gone a little overboard on the shopping today."

Again, that déjà-vu feeling struck her. He was handsome and poised and familiar—but why?

"I'm sorry, have we met before?" Oh, she did not just ask him that. It was her turn to blush now. She shaded her eyes with her hand. "I apologize. That sounded like a pickup line." Heat rushing through her core, she hurried to the cash register to help Clara with the growing line. There was no doubt that she was drawn to the man, but did she have to make it so obvious?

When she looked up from helping the last customer, Evan stood next to a life-size bear carved from burl and watched her. The way he grinned did pleasant things to her insides, a stark reminder of all she'd lost. Sela allowed that thought to douse cold water on her reaction to him.

Taking on a more serious tone, she edged around the counter and approached him. "Look, my question was inappropriate, and I didn't mean it like that anyway. It's just that you seem very familiar to me, like we've met before."

"We have, in the woods. Remember?"

"Funny. But I'm serious."

"I didn't mind the pickup line. Not at all." More ador-able grinning.

She smiled in spite of her attempt to avoid flirting. She didn't want to give him the wrong idea, but her efforts would come easier if only she didn't like him. "Look, I don't really know you. That wasn't my intention. Can we just forget that I said it?"

"No, we haven't met before the woods." His grin soft-ened to an understanding smile. "I would have remem-bered."

The guy was definitely still flirting, but on her cue, he'd turned it down a notch or two. Considerate of him.

Evan glanced at his watch, frowned then whipped out a credit card. "Would you mind charging the painting to this card. I'll come back to pick it up later. And please, if you would, let the furniture store know the desk has a buyer. I have an appointment, and I'm already late."

Sela went to the counter and wrote down the name of the furniture store where he could pick up his desk. She handed him the paper but refused the credit card. "I'll hold the painting for you. You can pay when you come back." Sela smiled and busied herself with de-cluttering the coun-ter. He made her nervous.

"Thank you. I appreciate that." Evan turned and strolled away. Halfway to the door he swung back around. "It was nice seeing you again, Sela."

She smiled in return—he flattered her with every look, it seemed. "You, too, Evan."

His grin left her floating.

After he was gone, Sela took a few deep breaths. She didn't know the man and was determined to know much more before she let her heart flutter away like it belonged to an adolescent.

* * *

Clara carried the painting over to the register and laid it on the counter. Sela gasped. In the painting, sunbeams broke through a mist-laden forest. Had he wanted to buy that painting because of the morning they'd met?

Clara cleared her throat. "At least you know he's coming back and you get to see him again."

"What do you mean?"

"Don't play dumb with me. I think you like him. He likes you, that's for sure."

"What in the world would give you that idea?" *Honestly.* Sela shook her head at Clara's assumption.

More than thirty years her senior, Clara was Sela's dearest friend, other than her sisters. Sela had attended church with her for years and David, too, when he was alive. She didn't know what she'd do without her wisdom and insight, but sometimes she overstepped. Problem was, Sela knew Clara was right. But she wasn't ready to admit anything, not even to herself.

"I've been around the block a few times, and I have eyes." Clara smiled. "And you've organized the pens and redwood magnets at least five times since he left."

Sela frowned. Had she betrayed David today? She'd guarded the love she'd had for David, their memories together, locking them inside her heart. While her head screamed it was time to move on, her heart was afraid of losing what little she had left.

And this man...this man had quickly and easily broken through her protective barrier—more like he'd jumped over it.

"Oh, now, don't go and do that. Stop beating yourself up. There's no crime in you being drawn to a man. Sela, honey, this is a good thing. A very good thing."

Chapter 3

Evan stood in the extra room of the condo belonging to Blackwood Development where he stayed while in California and stared at the too-large desk he'd purchased from Sela. The furniture store had delivered it late yesterday evening. Sela was right—the desk was impractical, but it had a rustic look that Evan liked. Still, the purchase had been impulsive. Just like his decision to see her again.

With a soft rag, he wiped off the desk and began setting up his home office—the project his father had dealt him would definitely require after-hours creativity and thought. He opened the top drawer and dumped in sticky pads, pencils, pens, staples. But then when he attempted to close it, it wouldn't budge. He tugged the drawer completely out to see if something had fallen into the empty space. He saw nothing. Evan tried the drawer once again but without success. He slipped his hand into the empty space and ran it along the top.

Evan felt the object. *What the...*

He pulled a small pistol from a holder secured in the desk. *Now that's odd.* He'd have to remember to return Sela's gun to her—though by the looks of it, it hadn't even been removed for years, to clean or otherwise. Maybe it belonged to the desk's previous owner.

He returned the pistol to its hiding place for the time being and repositioned the drawer, maneuvering it so that it would close.

A glance at his watch told him that he'd need to be at the Blackwood offices in forty-five minutes for a meeting with his father, who'd arrived home from a business trip late last night. He'd expect Evan's answer regarding Sela and her property. Unsure how best to address his father's divisive request, he sighed.

From what he could tell, Sela was a special woman. He wanted a chance to find out if there could be something between them. He hadn't believed the day would come when he'd want a serious relationship again. But after only two encounters with Sela, he found himself thinking along those lines.

At some point he'd have to tell her that his father owned Blackwood Development and was interested in purchasing her property. When he did, he would be completely aboveboard about it, but he had a feeling that he had to tread carefully. He didn't want her to believe his sudden appearance in her life had anything to do with persuading her to sell. And that was a problem, considering that it sort of did and considering his father's request.

How and when did he tell her the full truth of it?

If he told her now, he might destroy any chance he had. On the other hand, if he waited and told her later, he might destroy her trust in him at a juncture that would be more painful for both of them. Unless, of course, she understood the circumstances. It was a risk.

Someone knocked on the door.

At seven in the morning?

Evan tugged his crisp business shirt on and buttoned it on the way to the door. He wanted to dress the part for his meeting with his father today. A glance through the peephole sent dread through him.

Facing off with his father wasn't something he wanted to do before he'd had coffee. Evan swung the door open. "Dad, I figured I'd see you at the office."

His father strolled into the condo, dressed in his usual expensive business suit. Gone were the days when he was hands-on at the development worksites. These days he spent buying, selling, managing, and negotiating property. Impatience lingering behind his smile, he waved his hand in the air. "Morning's filled with too many meetings. Didn't think I'd get a chance to talk to you about this without interruption."

He peered around the condo. He had to notice that Evan hadn't personalized the place yet. Okay, well, there was the desk. Other than that, he had the one painting he'd purchased at Sela's shop and needed to pick up; he was saving that for the right time. He'd left most of his belongings behind in Virginia Beach until he could bring them, if necessary, including his guitar, which he hadn't taken time to play in…how long had it been anyway?

From where his father stood in the living room, Evan knew he could see the desk. Not good.

"Okay, what's up?" *As if I don't know.*

Instead of a reply, his father grinned and moved toward the extra bedroom. *Oh no. Here it comes.* He hadn't expected the man to show up at the condo.

His father strolled to the desk and ran his hand over the

smooth top. "You didn't happen across this at a burl gift shop, did you?"

Evan sighed. "Yes, I met her—if that's what you came by to find out."

His father studied him. "And?"

"And she's beautiful, just like you said. But there's more to her than that. You didn't play fair—you knew how I would react."

"All is fair in love and war."

Really, Dad? "We're talking about a human being with feelings here. I'm not going to use my charm, as you called it, to manipulate her the way you've suggested. Besides, she's too smart for that."

To Evan's surprise, his father rocked his head back with laughter. "I do believe you're smitten."

"I can't be. I hardly know her." *And I won't get a chance to know her if I'm not careful.* Reining in his emotions, Evan turned his back on his father and made his way behind the kitchen counter for some coffee. "I did what you asked, I met her, and now I'm giving you my decision. No."

The negative reply was the first he'd ever given his father. He sure hoped it was worth it. His hands trembled a little and made him spill some of the scalding coffee as he poured. *Ouch.* He quickly set the cup on the counter and ran cold tap water on his hand.

His father moved to the granite counter and stood across from him, scrutinizing. "What am I asking you to do that you aren't already doing? You're going to see her again, am I right?"

After adding some milk to cool the coffee, Evan downed the cup. He ground his molars, steadying his rising anger. "I've spent my entire life, from the moment I started working for you until now, groveling for every morsel, it seems. Working my way from the same starting point as a guy off the street with no education—a guy off the street who wasn't your son. I've worked hard to earn my own way in your company. Never have you asked me to manipulate someone like this." Was he actually going this far? "I can't. I won't. I already told you she won't fall for it."

"I see. You think you're above this." His father raised his chin. "Let me explain something. In every relationship, be it business or personal, people use each other—they manipulate and they persuade to obtain the outcome they want. That's a fact of life. This wouldn't be your first time. Think about it. Think about it hard before you become my greatest disappointment."

Evan's father turned and walked out of the condo.

Evan took the rest of the morning off. He simply couldn't face going into work or seeing his father. Not until he'd calmed down. Not until he'd figured things out. He strolled the beach near the Blackwood office, walking barefooted in the cold, moist sand. Each footstep pressed the water out of the sand and away from his foot. He watched, fascinated.

Mesmerized.

Approaching a pier where a lone fisherman sat with his fishing pole, Evan wiped off the sand and slipped his sneakers back on then continued to the farthest point, looking out on the ocean as he went.

If only he could put his foot down on the pain and regret in his heart and press them away. He doubted he would escape without disappointing his father—but when *hadn't* his father been disappointed?

Evan was still trying to get his approval.

Sela hung back on the small footbridge that crossed the Smith River and connected her property, giving Alexa some privacy with her new husband, Graeme. The two had only been married two years, and already they had one child and another on the way.

Sela had never imagined Alexa would be the type to have a child, much less two. Still, it warmed her heart to think that her sister had finally found someone to bring out the maternal instincts in her and to love her like a man should.

Alexa giggled and shoved Graeme in response to something he'd said. The two adored each other, and Sela found herself watching them, despite wanting to give them privacy. So much in love…

Sighing, she turned her attention to the river that flowed beneath her.

She was alone. Utterly alone. Looking across the way where the redwoods grew thick on her property, she thought back to the misty morning two weeks ago when she'd stumbled across Evan, or rather he'd stumbled across her. He'd come into the shop a week later and made arrangements to buy one of Camille's paintings and still hadn't picked it up.

A complete stranger, and yet Sela hoped she would see him again. During the week, she found herself looking up every time the doorbell signaled a customer entering her gift shop, her heart expectant, only to be disappointed when the customer wasn't Evan.

Was she that desperate? That lonely?

In the few moments she'd spent with him, both in the woods and in the store, he'd made her smile. Something in the way he'd looked at her touched a part of her deep inside. She shook off thoughts of Evan and crossed the bridge, passing Alexa and Graeme.

"Hey, Sela, wait up," Alexa called.

Sela stepped from the bridge onto the trail and turned

to watch Alexa as she hurried toward her, leaving Graeme. He headed in the opposite direction, presumably to take care of something work related.

Midway along in her second pregnancy, Alexa looked radiant and only showed a little. The couple had left their daughter, little Ricky, with a close friend while they took a few days for themselves with one caveat—Graeme had some unfinished business in the area, so they had stayed with Sela last night but were leaving today.

Alexa's breathing sounded a little fast, and upon reaching Sela she paused to catch her breath.

"Are you all right?" Sela asked.

"Of course. Never better. Graeme will be back in a few hours, so we have a little more time to catch up."

"Do you need to lie down for a while?" Sela steadied Alexa, who appeared dizzy for a second. "Maybe taking a walk right now isn't a good idea."

Alexa pressed her hand to her forehead, her face suddenly flushed. "You know, I think you're right. We can take a walk after I nap."

Sela pressed her hand against Alexa's back, guiding her onto the bridge.

Alexa shrugged away. "I'm not an invalid. Just a little tired, that's all."

And a little irritable, if you ask me. Sela decided to change the subject. "I'm so happy for you. It's seems magical how you met Graeme, and he really loves you. You two make the perfect couple. Though, next time you decide to take a few days for alone time, I'd love to have little Ricky stay with me." Sela smiled, hoping her hint didn't sound too pushy.

"We're only a couple hours away. You can come see us any time you want."

"I was lucky to get extra help with the shop this afternoon so we could spend time together." But Sela did need to find additional help. She wanted more freedom than the gift shop afforded her so that she could travel or watch little Ricky. Before the shop was hers, it had belonged to David's mother, Monica, and then David.

Her whole life seemed to revolve around taking care of what David had left behind. Still, she was grateful for what she had.

She should consider herself fortunate, as Evan had said when he'd first met her. But he hadn't known that she was a widow when he'd said it. He hadn't known the depth of her loneliness. How inadequate she felt compared to her talented, artistic sisters.

As they lumbered slowly across the bridge, Sela watched the endless flow of the peaceful river. Finally, they stepped from the bridge and started toward the house. She hoped all her sister needed was a nap. Since Sela had never been pregnant, she had no idea what to watch for in case Alexa had trouble.

Once inside Sela's home, Alexa went to the guest bedroom to lie down. Sela poured her a glass of water, and after a soft knock on the door, she peered in. Alexa was already resting in the bed but was still awake.

Sela pushed the door open all the way and entered the room. "Just in case you get thirsty." She set the glass down on the nightstand.

Alexa smiled as she rolled to her side and repositioned her pillow. "Thanks, sis. You can stay and talk, if you want."

"I thought you wanted a nap."

"Maybe in a bit. I thought with Graeme gone we would have some time alone." Alexa eyed Sela.

Sela knew that look, and considering her current frame of mind, she wasn't in the mood for probing questions. On the other hand, what could her sister be curious about that she didn't already know? Sela had nothing to hide.

"I hear there might be someone special in your life," Alexa said.

What in the world? Sela opened her mouth to speak but couldn't find the words and shut it. She shook her head then, "No, there's no one. Where did you hear that?"

Clara. Had to be—the older woman thought of herself as the grandmother Sela never had. That, or guardian angel. She hated the warmth that seemed to melt her cheeks. Maybe Alexa wouldn't notice, given that she was tired.

"Oh, pooh."

Sela couldn't help but smile at the change in Alexa since having her first child.

"I hoped it was true," Alexa said and yawned.

Frowning, Sela looked at her hands. She hated keeping something from Alexa, but there wasn't anything to talk about. Not yet. "I'm sorry."

Alexa closed her eyes, and Sela slipped out without another word.

In the kitchen she cleaned up the lunch dishes and made more coffee. Alexa wasn't the only one who was tired. Someone knocked softly on the front door. Graeme didn't need to knock before he came in, so it couldn't be him. She rushed around the counter, through the living room, and then to the foyer to open the door.

Evan filled her vision. Surprised, her heart swelled with warmth. Though her home was situated behind the gift shop, customers didn't usually show up at the door.

"Who is it, Sela?" Alexa called.

Before Sela could answer, her sister stood behind her. *I thought you were asleep.*

"Evan," Sela said, a little breathless. "What are you doing here?"

Chapter 4

What am *I doing here?*

Seeing Sela again—her soft, warm smile, deep blue eyes, and auburn hair—his mind went blank. The well-thought-out explanation he'd prepared slipped away.

He cleared his throat, recovering. "I…uh…I wanted to thank you for holding the painting for me."

Her smile grew wide. He could tell she was glad to see him, and he relaxed a little, although he was expecting her to be alone. Another woman stood just behind Sela, and Evan knew instantly that they were sisters.

"Won't you come in?" Her sister stepped forward, one hand pressed to her belly, revealing she was pregnant.

Evan didn't miss the look Sela gave her, so he hesitated. "I didn't mean to intrude. I just…" *wanted to see you again.* He was pathetic. He waited for Sela's invitation.

"Yes, Evan. Please, come in." She smiled.

He couldn't help but be drawn to the gentle, lovely creature she was. Nor could he imagine she'd ever spoken a rude word in her life. That's why he wasn't positive she really wanted him in her home. But how could he say no? This is what he'd hoped for, wasn't it? At every turn, he felt more and more like he was scheming his way into her life, despite his intentions otherwise.

"If you're sure I'm not intruding," he said, offering her a questioning look, a chance to renege.

"Of course not," she said.

Her sister quickly grabbed his elbow and ushered him inside, surprising him. She was a more forceful person than Sela, that much was obvious.

"Evan, this is my sister, Alexa."

"It's a pleasure." Evan thrust his hand out to shake Alexa's—a business-world habit.

"Very nice to meet you," she said, taking his hand. Her grip was firm. After she released it, she gave an exaggerated yawn. "I don't mean to be rude, but I think I'm going back to my nap, sis, if that's all right."

A look of concern crossed Sela's face. "Are you sure you're feeling okay? Should I call Graeme?"

"No. I just need a very long nap, and having to reassure Graeme won't get me there." She smiled and looked from Evan back to Sela. "Nice to meet you, Evan." Alexa disappeared down the hallway.

Evan returned his attention to Sela, though it had never really left.

"Can I get you something to drink?" Sela glanced out the window before her gaze settled back on him. "Coffee or tea?"

"Is my being here awkward for you? I realize that your sister is the one who initially invited me inside. Maybe that's not what *you* wanted." His words were a little forward, but being transparent with her from the start, as much as possible, was what he wanted. Was for the best. No point in playing games.

Someone always lost when games were played.

A pretty pink spread over her cheeks, and at that moment, with her face framed by her auburn hair, she was the picture of perfection.

"Evan…"

She feels uncomfortable. His heart missed a beat.

"It's a little awkward." Her smile was gentle, reassuring. "But not for the reason you might think. I'm glad you're here. I've…wanted to see you again."

He grinned, feeling it to his toes. "Then, sure. I'll have something. Whatever you're having."

"Make yourself comfortable, then." She disappeared into the kitchen.

Evan blew out a breath and took a seat at the edge of a navy leather sofa. His palms slicked. He felt like he was on his first date with her—which was far from true—but maybe that's because he wanted this to count. If only he didn't have his father's request weighing on him. Somehow, he needed to get that out in the open, and fast.

Get it behind them.

A glance around the room revealed snippets of life with her late husband. Then he noticed a guitar hanging on the wall here and there. He moved to one of the beautiful handmade creations. The top wood was a bright reddish brown.

Redwood…

Light-gauge strings. Evan's pulse quickened. He'd never seen a guitar made with redwood, but he'd heard that redwood used for tone wood made a powerful, finger-style tone with lots of brilliance and clarity—perfect for classical guitar.

He thought to slide his hand across the smooth, silky grain—

"Before he died my husband made custom, handcrafted guitars." Sela's voice startled him from behind.

Evan snatched his hand back like he'd been caught sneaking a piece of pie before dinner. He turned in time to see Sela's knowing look as she set a tray with a carafe, mugs, sugar, and cream on the table. That was fast. The coffee must have already been made.

"He taught me what he knew, and on occasion I'll make one upon request," she said.

That news impressed Evan. "Did you make this one? The craftsmanship is amazing. And the tone wood is an interesting combination. I'm curious about how this would sound. What playing style and technique does it complement?"

She studied him, surprise mingled with suspicion in her intense blue eyes. He knew what she was thinking—it wasn't every day a person met someone who knew about guitars—specifically how different woods fit together to create certain tones. Evan was a little taken aback himself that her husband knew such things. Made guitars.

"No, the few I've made were commissioned and are with the owners."

"That makes sense." Evan chuckled. "This one your husband made but not upon request, then?"

"He made it for himself." She slowly sat on the sofa, her soft smile remaining, despite her serious expression. "I take it you play?"

He gestured toward the guitar. "Yes. What about you? I'd love to hear you."

Sela shook her head—as if unable to speak what she was really thinking—and poured the coffee, her hands shaking slightly. "Not really. David had all the talent. You're welcome to try the guitar."

An emotion he couldn't read flitted across her features

and then, just as quickly, it was gone. What was it—displeasure? Resentment? Or had Evan imagined it? Had no one since her late husband touched this guitar? Was that why he'd seen momentary distress in her eyes?

Though hesitant because of her reaction, Evan hoped to remedy that and lifted the guitar from the hook. He sat on the ottoman near him, cradling the guitar in his lap, and ran his fingers over the strings, surprised to find that it was already tuned. Then an image flashed in his mind.

Sela…in the mist…holding a guitar. This guitar. He hadn't remembered until that moment, probably because he'd been so enamored with meeting her. Deep down, in some old-fashioned way, Evan realized he wanted a chance to serenade her.

Closing his eyes, he drew in a deep breath. He hoped Sela would enjoy his performance. If she did, then years of classical guitar lessons when he was growing up hadn't been for nothing.

He'd start with a classical tune. If she was familiar with classical at all, she would have heard it. It had been so long since he'd played, could he even do it justice? Or would he simply make a fool of himself?

He began slowly, plucking two strings then scaled the chords moving into a smooth *accelerando*, or a gently quickening pace. But his fingers had grown soft, losing the calluses. He ignored the friction against his fingertips and played for Sela. He wouldn't back off, allowing the music to fill his ears, his heart, and to flow through him.

Connecting him with Sela.

"Capricho Árabe…"

Written by Francisco Tárrega, one of the great Spanish composers.

Sela stared at Evan unable to comprehend that he was playing David's guitar.

Classical music.

On David's classical guitar.

Despite her effort to protect her heart, the music overwhelmed her. She closed her eyes, listening to talent she hadn't heard in years. Not since David was alive. She hated the moisture that crept into the corner of her eyes.

No. She would not cry. She couldn't reveal to Evan the effect his music had on her. Yet her body trembled, and if he looked closely, he would see. She could feel the emotion in his music as he poured even more into the classical song, into each string he plucked, each chord he strummed.

Sela let go, if only a little. She allowed the music, this man, to serenade her. To draw near the deepest part of her heart. Near the place where she'd kept David.

Something inside shifted. Evan Black—a stranger by all accounts—was stirring things inside that had died with her husband.

Opening her eyes, she watched him—his handsome face and lean, athletic form—as he continued to play. He shut his eyes, appearing to ride on the notes. The way his hands moved up and down the neck, the way his fingers moved quickly, held her captive. His mouth was closed but moved slightly, humming along with the song, she guessed, though too softly for her to hear him above the guitar.

Her gaze fell on his lips. No…what was the matter with her?

Emotions rippled through her. Joy, passion, and peace mesmerized her. Sela needed to rein in her feelings before it was too late, but she was already in trouble.

Then he began to rock back and forth, subtle at first, but his body moved with the music.

A familiar mannerism. David used to do the same thing. In the same way.

Sela slowly stood and slipped her hand to her throat. When she'd first seen him in the mist, her first impression had been of David. And then again in the gift shop, with the way he'd tilted his head, another familiar mannerism.

And now as he played… Sela's pulse almost drowned out Evan's music. He'd given her that déjà-vu feeling all along, but she knew why now.

David! He reminded her too much of David.

What was going on? Who was this man? Was Sela going crazy? "Stop," she said, softly at first, then louder. "Stop it!"

Evan's eyes immediately flew open, and the music stalled to a deafening silence. He appeared jarred from a distant land. Just as Sela had been. But now she was back in reality, or was she?

"Who are you?"

Caught up in the music, Evan was stunned by the interruption. Gathering his thoughts took a few seconds. "I got carried away. I'm sorry."

He stood then because Sela was standing. Although he didn't know her well, he never imagined he'd see her dark frown or the accusation in her eyes. And it wasn't his imagination this time. Nor was it fading. Why had she reacted so strongly? He'd thought she would enjoy the music.

"Who are you?" Her voice bordered on forceful, belying the soft-spoken woman he'd known so far. "Really?"

Evan sagged. She must already know the truth about him, then. The ruse was up—a ruse he'd never intended. Though how his playing the guitar had somehow helped her to connect him to Blackwood Development, to his father, he didn't know.

Gathering his composure, he put the guitar back on the wall. What would he, could he say? Was it possible to make her understand? To explain his way out of this?

Drawing in a defeated breath, he turned to face her. Her eyes grew dark against a pale face. If only he could go to her now and wrap his arms around her. Make everything right.

"Look." He held out his palms. "I never meant to hurt you."

"Tell me now. Who are you, and what do you want?"

"It's not what you think." Evan hesitated, searching for the words, hating that he'd waited before telling her the whole truth. If only he had told her from the beginning. "I like you and simply want to get to know you. This has nothing to do with—"

A framed snapshot on the wall behind Sela jarred him, interrupting his next words. He hadn't seen it before because he was sitting on the sofa, the photograph behind him. He took a shaky step forward.

Sela was the one who had some explaining to do.

"Why do you have a picture of my father hanging on your wall?"

Chapter 5

The angry tenor in Evan's voice sent a sliver of fear through her.

What, really, did she know about this man? And how dare he use that tone with her? If anyone should be incensed, it was Sela, though she'd never had cause to experience the emotions bombarding her. She didn't know how to respond.

What to do?

His father? The meaning behind his question finally hit her. Evan stood near her, examining the picture of David's father. She peered at the image, too. A handsome man in his thirties, early forties maybe, stared back.

"What do you mean that it's a picture of your father?" She asked the question, but already the similarities were sifting through the fog in her mind.

"My father...why do you have this picture of him?"

"David's mother gave this to him—it's a picture of *his* father. He never met the man."

Sela strolled across the room and touched the guitar Evan had just played, the strings still warm. "That explains so much," she said, her voice barely a whisper. Her odd familiarity with Evan—his mannerisms, the similarities in his appearance, and his musical talent. It all made sense now.

Evan remained frozen, staring. Stricken and hurt didn't describe his expression.

Her heart went out to him. "Evan…" She approached him and touched his arm, wanting to comfort him but not knowing how.

He didn't move, didn't respond, as though he hadn't heard her, had forgotten she was there, hadn't felt her touch. This must be more of a shock to him than it was to her. So David had a brother. Confusion ripped through her leaving shards of pain, anger, and resentment. Had David known and kept this from her?

No. She wasn't thinking straight. David hadn't known any more than Evan had. That much was obvious.

"Did you know?" His voice strained, Evan kept his focus on the picture.

"That David had a brother? No. I'm sure he didn't, either. Oh Evan, I'm so sorry." Again, she brushed her hand along his upper arm, empathizing with his pain. "But don't you see, that's why I was so upset just now."

For the first time since laying eyes on the photo, Evan pulled his haggard gaze away. He pinned her with his eyes. In them she saw a battle raging. What was he thinking?

When he didn't reply, Sela continued. "I haven't heard anyone play like you did just now since…well, since my husband. So many other things about you have given me this eerie sense that I knew you. That we'd met before. Just now, listening to you on the guitar, I realized how much you reminded me of David, and it scared me. I couldn't imagine why you would suddenly turn up in my life and use his mannerisms, play his guitar—it was too much to be a coincidence. It was like you wanted to torment me. I know it sounds crazy. And yet, you're not twins. David was older than you are, if only by a few years."

"That's just it, Sela." He set the photo down on the table next to the sofa instead of hanging it back on the wall. "It's not a coincidence that I'm here. My stepping into your life is no accident."

His tormented gaze held hers. So, he'd sought her out on purpose? He had ulterior motives for meeting her in the woods, his purchases at her shop, and stopping by here today?

Sela frowned, hating the nausea his statement caused to churn in her stomach. "No accident?"

"Remember that first morning that you found me on your property?" Evan's hands were secured in his pockets, and he watched her from beneath concerned brows.

"You weren't lost?" Remembering that morning, remembering that she'd wanted to see the handsome stranger again, Sela's throat grew tight. "That was no accident? You weren't lost but were there to meet me?" She could hardly croak out the question. *But why?*

"I'm not communicating very well." He tugged a hand from his pocket and scratched his chin. The same war still waging in his dark eyes, Sela sensed that somehow he managed to steady his composure for her sake. That he was the injured party here. That he was in more turmoil than she. Still, if he'd purposefully wormed his way into her life, into her home today…she wasn't certain who should be the angry one.

She huffed, arching a brow. "I'm listening."

"I was definitely lost, but I'd been walking the property lines, looking at your property specifically. The mist threw me off, and that's when you found me wandering on the wrong side of the line."

An ache grew between her temples. She pressed her hand against her forehead. "I'm confused. You say that your appearance was no accident, that you were looking at my property, and yet you didn't know that David was your brother? What is going on?"

"You and I have both suffered an injustice, Sela. Before I go any further, let me tell you that I'm here today because I wanted to see you again. Nothing else that I'm about to tell you has any bearing on that. Do you believe me?"

The walls swirled around her. Sela slowly sank into the sofa. "I hardly know you well enough, Evan." *Besides, you're David's brother....*

Sela looked away from his intense, pleading gaze. She had a feeling that she was about to wish she'd never met the man. Why had David's long-lost brother suddenly turned up interested in property belonging to a brother he didn't know he had? Or at least, belonging to his brother's widow.

Evan squeezed his fists, restraining the anger and hurt roiling inside.

He struggled to comprehend the news. A brother?

I have...no, had *a brother. A brother I never had the chance to know.*

David was gone. The conniving father they shared had lied to Evan his whole life. Probably to the both of them. Had David known or suspected anything? Had his father waited until after David died to approach his widow? The extent of his deception was beyond comprehension.

Evan rubbed his hand down his face and remembered

where he was. Sela sat watching him. He should leave her alone and address his father now, but this might be his last chance with...his late brother's wife. He reeled to think of her in those terms.

No matter that he'd wanted to spend time with her, get to know her. For his late brother's sake, for David's sake, he needed to set things right.

Where and how did he begin to explain this to her? He inhaled in an effort to slow his racing heart, dark rage turning in his stomach. "David's father..." Evan squeezed his eyes shut, "*my* father..." then he opened them again and watched Sela's anxious face.

He'd gone against that niggling that told him to stay away. He knew it would end badly. But never could he have imagined the cause. And for that reason, he couldn't blame his father alone for this—Evan was just as much to blame. He'd done this to her. "My father is Robert Black, the man who owns Blackwood Development—the company that wants to buy your property."

"And that's why it's no accident you're here. You knew who I was all along." Betrayal laced her hostile tone.

Oddly, her eyes begged him to prove her wrong. And he would, if given half a chance. "Yes and no." Evan paced the room as he searched for the words. How much of the full, unadulterated truth could she handle right now? "I was asked to befriend you, persuade you to sell."

Sela gasped, her hand sliding to her throat.

Great. That was not the best place to start.

He knew he had but seconds before she threw him out. "I agreed to nothing, except to walk the property line. And, I agreed to meet you, but I never agreed to anything more. When I met you, I really liked you. I wanted to get to know you for personal reasons. But my father's request hung over my head, and I knew I needed to tell you soon.

"I had hoped to find a way to tell you who I am today, so that you would know from the beginning. I'm just sorry we couldn't have met under other circumstances. It was never my intention to hurt or manipulate you." That was everything he knew to say.

Would she understand? Believe him? Or had he already lost all trust? Evan risked a glimpse at her, fearing he'd see rejection. But he only saw confusion, the struggle to understand—the same things warring inside him.

She needed time to absorb everything before she knew what to think. Like Evan needed time to comprehend that he'd had a brother and his father never told him.

Evan stopped pacing and looked at the floor, guilt weighing heavily on his shoulders. "I'm sorry that I didn't have the chance to know David. I…"

"Evan…"

Resentment pulsating through every cell, Evan couldn't contain it anymore. He had to confront his father. He stalked from the room and headed to the door, not looking back at Sela. He couldn't take hearing how she must feel at the news he'd just shared. Anything she said would slash at an already open, bleeding wound.

Besides, she needed time, and he'd give her that. He reached for the door.

"Evan, wait." Sela placed her hand on his arm. Her tender touch sent warmth curling around his bitterness. How could she show mercy? Life would crush a soul that kindhearted.

He stared at his hand on the doorknob. Any words he might have said wouldn't come—he'd said enough already as it was. Instead, he shook his head, resentment squeezing his throat, strangling him. He couldn't breathe. "I have to get out of here."

* * *

Sela stood frozen, staring at the closed door, all Evan's words whirling in her mind like a vortex, sucking her down. Deep.

Seeing his anguish, she'd forsaken her own and tried to soothe his pain. After all, it was his father who had betrayed them all.

Finally alone in the room, Sela allowed her tumultuous emotions to crash down on her. "So…Evan is David's half brother…." She mumbled the words to herself.

Somehow, she found her way to a chair in the small foyer. If she could have made it, she would have gone to the river, but she feared her shaking legs would give out. At the river, the lull of the moving water might have comforted her soul and washed the feelings of betrayal far away. Might have…

Pressing her face into her hands, she wanted to sob all the pain away, but her eyes were dry. Still, she cried, her shoulders shaking, without shedding a tear.

Lord, I thought You sent Evan. She'd allowed herself a sliver of hope that there could be something more between them. For the first time since David's death, she had wanted that. She had looked forward to the possibilities.

Disappointment wrangled with betrayal—how could she feel anything romantic for Evan now? There was too much hanging over their heads.

Falling for David's brother like that was just…out of the question.

A hand squeezed her shoulder. "Sis, are you okay?"

Sela looked up into Alexa's concerned eyes, glad her sister was there. She needed a lifeline.

Chapter 6

For now, at least, the Blackwood offices took up the second floor of the First Citizens Bank building. His father was already drawing up the plans to build a permanent regional office building—a Blackwood showcase—in the region.

In the parking lot, Evan sat in his Tahoe. He wasn't sure if he should calm down first, ensuring he spoke his mind coherently, or if he should release all the pent-up anger he harbored toward his father.

Adding to his torture were his last words to Sela. They should have been more reassuring. Instead, his anger had won out and he'd left her standing there to deal with the news. At least with her sister there, she wouldn't have to process it alone.

The whole situation was a complete outrage. Minutes ticked by before Evan could muster his nerve. Facing off with his father wasn't something to be taken lightly, no matter his father's sins.

Evan pounded the steering wheel before slipping from the vehicle. Before he knew it, he stood before his father's closed door, his mind so preoccupied with the matters at hand he didn't register that he'd made the walk from his vehicle to this point. Voices resounded inside the office.

He took a deep breath and grabbed the doorknob—

"Oh, Evan, I'm sorry." Michelle, his father's secretary, approached from behind. She'd been absent from her desk moments before. "Your father is meeting with Senator Carmichael."

Of course. "This is more important," he said, steeling his nerves. Then he opened the door and strode toward his father, breaking into an already heated discussion.

Robert Black was practiced in measuring his reaction, taking things in stride. Though his eyes flared with indignation, he remained calm and smiled as if Evan had not just committed a major faux pas. "Evan, I'd like for you to meet Senator—"

"Tell me about my brother." Evan never glanced at the senator, not wanting to risk losing the forward momentum of his ire.

His father's smile faltered, and he glanced at the senator then rose. He ushered the politician to the door. Evan didn't turn around and watch the men but imagined his father thrusting his hand out at that moment.

"Thank you for stopping by, Jim. You'll have my numbers on your desk by next week. Will that do?"

The words were smooth as honey, like Evan hadn't just been rude to an important person.

Taking everything in stride.

Robert Black should run for office. He had the gifts required by most politicians these days. Evan made no move to look behind him; he simply listened to the exchange. Finally, the click of the door shutting resounded, cutting through the silent tension.

The confrontation imminent, his breaths came quicker.

His father said nothing as he strolled from the closed door back to his desk. Evan kept his eyes focused ahead until his father slid back into view.

"I had a brother, and you never told me."

"You were rude to the senator just now."

"Why?" Pain burned behind Evan's eyes. He hated that he was beginning to falter. "Why did you lie to me, to David, and to your daughter-in-law?" What kind of person would do that? That Evan's father was such a person cut to the marrow.

"You're judging me before you have the facts."

Would the man's gloves ever come off? Because Evan was prepared to have it out. But no, he just sat there and swiveled back and forth in his leather executive chair, bouncing the eraser end of a pencil. A nervous act Evan had never seen his father do.

"Let's have the facts then, and see if you're without guilt."

"Don't speak to me with disrespect. Neither as my employee nor as my son." Robert leveled his gaze on Evan, who met it with equal severity. "How did you find out?" his father asked.

Evan scoffed. "I hardly think that matters."

"Until you, I was the only living person who knew about David. How did you find out?"

"Did you really think you could keep something like that a secret? I saw a picture of you on the wall while at Sela's home. A simple snapshot, Dad. That's all it took to bring out the truth. You were much younger, but I've seen pictures of you when you were young. In fact, I've seen that *exact* picture of you, so I recognized you immediately. What did you think would happen when you sent me after her?"

For a fleeting moment, the slice of a grin slipped into his father's lips, but his frown shoved it away. If he knew anything of his father's actions lately, he'd guess the man was happy to hear that Evan had made it that far in his relationship with Sela. Evan clenched his fists, shame and regret squeezing his chest like a vise at the way he felt about his own father. And any chance of a friendship with Sela was destroyed.

"All right, Evan. I admit I might not have handled the situation very well. But you need to calm down and hear me out."

Evan remained standing, seething.

"I'll tell you everything if you'll have a seat. You're not going to stand over me like some judge putting me on trial."

What choice did Evan have if he wanted to hear the truth? He slipped into the still-warm chair opposite his father's desk where the senator had previously sat.

"David's mother and I weren't married, but after she left me, I spent over a decade looking for her. When I found her, I discovered I had a son." His father stared across the desk at Evan as though waiting for his words to sink in.

They did. "Were you married to Mom? Or were you having an affair?" A brick dropped in his gut.

"No. I wasn't married to your mother—didn't even know her then—when I was with Monica, David's mother. But I never told her about them."

"Why not? Why didn't you at least tell me or Sela? Why hide everything? Especially after Mom died, you wouldn't have had to worry about hurting her."

"Because…" His father raised his voice and stood. "Because," softer now, "I wasn't part of his life. Monica refused to let me be involved—after all, she'd left me. She had her reasons. After I heard that she'd died, I wanted to approach David. But by then David was happily married."

Evan had never seen the man pace. The action spoke volumes about his father's turmoil. Still, Evan needed more information.

Scratching his chin, Evan pictured his father doing the same. They shared that mannerism. Apparently, mannerisms were as much genetic as they were environmental, if Sela had seen things in Evan's actions that reminded her of David.

"Dad, why didn't you tell him that you were his father?" With his words, Evan found that some of his resentment had faded.

"I struggled with what to do, but having a father you never met suddenly appear in your life is disruptive at best. He…they…were so happy together. What could I add to the equation except grief?" Robert shook his head. "No, I did the right thing, staying away."

Right. Save the grief for later. For me. For Sela. "I can understand all that, although I don't agree with your decision. But what I can't understand is why you then try to buy Sela's land without disclosing your true identity, and then you send me—David's half brother—to woo his widow in order to charm her out of her land." Evan found himself standing. He faced his father now, the gloves off.

"Because by all rights that land belongs to me."

Was his father losing his grip with reality? Evan grimaced. "No. It belongs to Sela. Just leave her alone."

A knock came at the door, and Michelle peered inside. "I'm terribly sorry to interrupt, but if we're going to meet Mr. Saxon, we need to go."

His father appeared to snap out of his weighty mood

along with their conversation, brushing Evan aside like an annoying insect. "Let him know we're on our way."

Mr. Saxon must be an important client, prospect, or someone who had the power to influence California land permits. That his father hadn't included Evan was just as well. Evan was in no mood, considering the torrent of dark thoughts swirling in his mind.

None of what his father said, even if he believed the land belonged to him, explained his manipulative tactics. His father wasn't giving full disclosure—which begged the question, what was he hiding?

Whatever was going on, Evan should stay away from Sela. Falling for a woman who'd been married to a half brother Evan never knew about was—he swallowed the knot swelling in his throat—more than he could stomach.

"Are you sure you're going to be okay?" Alexa stood next to the family minivan that Graeme had purchased for their growing family, trading in his dilapidated old Jeep.

After her long nap yesterday, Alexa had stumbled in on the end of Sela's conversation with Evan, and the news left her as upset as Sela. Her sister had given her a few minutes to herself and then was there at her side to comfort her.

Thank goodness rest had restored Alexa to her normal, exhilarated self. Sela was grateful that her sister was there when she needed her.

Ignoring her pounding headache, Sela forced a smile. "Of course. You didn't have to stay another night just for me."

Alexa peered inside the van where Graeme waited in the driver's seat. "We can stay longer, or I can stay longer if you need me. Or you can pack up and come stay with us."

"Come on, you're practically newlyweds still. You need your privacy." Sela feigned a yawn in the early morning dawn. "And besides, I need time alone to think things through."

Her sister's expression grew stern. "I don't want you to see that man right now. I don't trust him. Let the dust settle. Call me, and we'll talk."

"I'm not sure it'll be that easy to avoid him. We're connected now."

Frowning, Alexa squeezed Sela's forearm. "I hoped there could have been more between you two, you know that, but now…you should stay away from him. At least for a while. Give it some time."

A myriad of contradictory feelings whirled through Sela's mind and heart. "I can't think straight about any of it. But Graeme's been really patient to let you guys stay one more night. You should probably get going now."

Her beautiful, glowingly pregnant sister glimpsed inside the van at her husband. "You're probably right."

She hugged her sister and slipped into the minivan. Sela watched them back out of her small drive, past her secluded gift shop, and onto the road. Then the minivan disappeared into another foggy morning.

Sela tugged her light jacket around her, the weight of her discovery pressing in on her like the mist. Of course, the morning would have to remind her of Evan—as if she could stop thinking about him. The look on his face. The fact that he was David's brother. That their father had wanted Evan—if Evan had been telling the truth, if he could be trusted—to hopefully persuade Sela to sell her land.

Had Evan been on that path? Had he agreed? His actions said that he had—he'd appeared at the shop and made plans to buy the desk and painting. Then he'd come to her house. But the shock and realization, the betrayal she'd seen in his eyes told her differently.

Making her way across the footbridge, she walked deep into the woods, as she had two weeks ago when she'd first met Evan. The mist-shrouded forest wrapped around her, hiding her. She picked her way along the familiar path and finally sank on a stump to rest.

Lord, I thought...I thought there was a chance that with Evan You were answering the ache in my heart, telling me to let my husband go. So I could move on. And now...

Sela didn't know what to think. She recalled that a representative for the development company had approached her on two different occasions to discuss purchasing the property. At the time, she was in no frame of mind to let go of all she had left of her husband. But now, she almost wished she had sold it and been done with it.

"Sela…"

A familiar voice whispered her name. Sela bolted from the stump and listened, waiting. Then she saw Evan a few yards away. He headed toward her.

Seeing him again, the shock of learning David had a half brother and that said brother had stormed into her life in an attempt to charm her and convince her to sell her acreage, washed over her anew.

"I see you found your way onto my property again." Sela never thought it hard to smile until today. *Careful, this is David's brother.* "Are you still stalking me?" The harsh words felt wrong.

Evan's already remorseful expression grew more somber. "I came here to think. And yes, I had hoped to see you, but I didn't count on it."

Sela said nothing. She wasn't sure she could trust him, and yet her need to believe in him ran deep.

Evan took a few more steps in her direction until he stood only three feet from her. Sela was drawn to the man, despite the intolerable circumstances. Alexa's words ignited in her mind. *"Stay away from him."*

"I came here to be alone, to think things through. I see I no longer have any privacy."

"You're wrong. After today, you'll never see me again. I only wanted to see you one last time. To let you know how sorry I am about what happened."

Sela regretted her harsh words. Evan had suffered a father's betrayal in the worst possible way. Unless his father didn't know…but no, that was impossible. The man knew all right, and despite his father, Evan didn't deserve the way she lashed out at him.

"I'm sorry for not telling you who I was up front. I wanted to, had planned to, but I wanted to get to know you, too. It's just…it all blew up before I had an opportunity to explain." Evan looked at the redwood needles on the forest floor.

That all made sense—if it was true. "Explain it to me now."

"What?"

"Pretend that none of this happened, and tell me what you were going to tell me. Start from that moment when I questioned who you were. You stopped playing the guitar."

Evan stared at her, and then a small grin lifted the corner of his right cheek. "Could we back up a little to a point before I played the guitar? I meant to tell you before you reacted like that. But then, I couldn't have expected your reaction because I didn't know what we would both discover later."

Despite everything, Sela couldn't help but smile. Evan was endearing, like his brother, but he wasn't David. He was completely different. She took comfort in that thought. "Okay, start over at the day like today when you ran into me here in the woods."

The way Evan nodded she could tell he didn't like that as an option, either. "Excuse me, miss."

"Oh, you're on my property, you must be lost," she said, playing along and laughing at the stilt to her words.

"You must be Sela Fox. It's a pleasure to meet you," Evan said and thrust out his hand.

Sela hesitated then slowly reached out and grasped his hand, his grip warm and sturdy. She released it. "Yes, that's me, and you are?"

"My name is Evan Black. My father owns Blackwood Development…. Hold on," Evan scratched his head. "This isn't the way I would have told you, either."

Sela arched a brow.

"Yesterday, when I came to your home I had hoped the opportunity would present itself. Here goes. Sela, I like you a lot, but there's something I want to get out in the open. My father is Robert Black of Blackwood Development. He sent me to investigate your property—a property he wants to buy. I agreed only to look into things, but after meeting you I realized that I would like to get to know you on a more personal level, outside of any business dealings. I'm sorry that I didn't identify myself at the outset, but I wasn't sure how to approach you."

"That wasn't so hard, was it?"

He let out a pent-up breath. "What would you have said, Sela?"

"I appreciate your honesty, Evan, and while I do believe you, it's impossible to extricate that the reason you met me in the first place has everything to do with your and David's father. I can't…I don't have an answer."

Evan frowned. "You're right, of course."

"But I can tell you that I like you, too. I would have enjoyed getting to know you better." Sela's throat hitched at the words.

"And I only came here to find you and tell you I'm sorry things worked out the way they did. Don't worry. I have every intention of staying away from you, keeping my father away from you. It's for your own good. So you don't need to worry about running into me in the woods, your store, or your house."

Then Evan Black turned and disappeared in the mist. The thought of never seeing him again unsettled her like nothing else that had happened. She hadn't expected his words of finality, ending their friendship before it started.

Hadn't expected the hot ache behind her eyes or the wrenching pain in her heart.

Chapter 7

Camille's painting of the sunbeams breaking through a mist-laden redwood forest stared back at Sela. The painting rested against the wall in the back room of her store, waiting for the man she held it for to claim it.

"He was all set to get it a couple a days ago. I don't know what happened," Clara said.

I do. This was awkward. "Did he pay you for it?" Sela asked.

"Not yet. He wanted to thank you for holding it, and I was happy to tell him where he could find you." Clara patted Sela's back. "I'm sorry, dear. I hope I didn't overstep."

"No worries, Clara. I'm going to deliver this myself."

Clara shot her a knowing grin.

Maybe that was because Sela hadn't yet shared the stunning news with her about David's brother. She simply couldn't find the right words. In that way, she better understood Evan's difficulty telling her the truth as well.

Sela peeled out of her work apron. "You mind watching the shop this afternoon?"

"Of course not." Clara winked. The woman would likely have taken on an unusually crowded store if it meant Sela was out spending time with a romantic interest.

After she wrapped the painting for delivery, Sela looked up the Blackwood office address, stuffed the painting in the back of her decades-old Suburban, and headed out.

The second Evan made his pronouncement that she would never see him again, she'd known she couldn't abide by that. If nothing else was between them, Evan and his father were still David's only living family.

David would have loved his brother had he been alive. He would have forgiven him anything, forgiven his father as well. He was that kind of person. Should she be any different? Sure, Robert Black had been devious, and she should watch herself when around him, but it wasn't her place to judge the man for his misdeeds.

It was her place to pray for him.

And as for Evan, she believed he was sincere when he said he never intended to manipulate her. Nor would she have fallen for that, so the very idea seemed a stretch at best. She believed that he was genuinely interested in getting to know her.

And she returned that interest.

Still…he was David's brother. She had to let any other ideas about Evan go, didn't she? Thoughts of a deeper friendship with him had nothing at all to do with why she steered her vehicle through town to Blackwood Development's offices.

Nothing at all.

Taking the painting to him felt good. Right. It would be her gift to Evan. Her way of saying all was forgiven.

Sela made her way through the lobby of the bank building, holding the painting. She rode the elevator up to the
second floor and stepped into a plush foyer with a receptionist.

"I'm here to deliver and hang a painting for Evan
Black." Sela smiled, hoping to disarm the receptionist,
hoping she'd have the chance to hang the painting. She'd
have to return to her Suburban and grab the toolbox she
always carried.

The receptionist hesitated as two calls came through at
the same time. "His office is down that hall, second door
to your left."

The receptionist smiled and began answering the phone.

"Thank you," Sela said. But the receptionist had already
answered the phone and shoved Sela from her thoughts.
She had always marveled that phone calls seemed to be
more important than a person standing there in the flesh.

She carefully lugged the four-foot-tall painting down
the long hallway. But as the walls closed in around her,
her decision to come here today, give Evan the painting,
seemed impulsive. The bounce in her step lessened. Evan
might not be happy to see her. Maybe his pronouncement
was as much for him as it had been for her.

In fact, now that she reconsidered her decision to appear
unannounced at his office, Sela decided Evan would be
displeased. But then again, she hadn't come here to make
him happy. She admitted she'd needed an excuse to make
an appearance at Blackwood so she could present her case
to both Evan and his father.

Sela hesitated at the doorway of Evan's office until she
was sure it was empty. She wanted to surprise him with
the painting hung on the wall. She crept inside and began
unwrapping it. She could grab her tool kit afterward. There

was only one place the painting would hang well, so it wasn't like his opinion was needed.

Voices in the hallway grew louder, and regret choked Sela.

Maybe this wasn't such a good idea.

Moisture slicked her palms, and her finger stung from a paper cut as she unwrapped the painting.

"What the…" Evan's surprise was palpable.

Sela turned to face him. Robert Black—CEO of Blackwood Development and David and Evan's father—stood just behind Evan, his frame filling the doorway. The resemblance between the two—between the *three*—was uncanny.

His grin spread wide, and he looked from Evan to Sela. "Well, Mrs. Fox, this is a pleasant surprise."

Sela smiled in return, though everything inside her said she needed to bolt. To run from this man.

"What are you doing here?" Evan finally recovered enough to speak.

"I brought your painting. Thought I'd hang it for you."

"I haven't paid for that yet."

"I know. It's a gift."

Evan came all the way into his office, frowning. "You shouldn't be here."

Sela could sense the words pained him. She returned her attention to ripping the rest of the paper off.

Moving to her side, he grabbed her hand to stop her progress. "Sela, what are you doing?"

Evan held her gaze, and the warm concern in his eyes caressed her wary, lonely heart. She'd been brave this far. With a little assurance, she could keep going with her plan. "You're all the family David had left. I want to get to know you. I think he would have wanted that."

After releasing her hand, he studied her. A light flickered in his dark eyes, drawing Sela deeper. She'd come here, convincing herself this was an attempt to honor her deceased husband. But now she wasn't so sure about her reasons.

"This isn't a good idea," he said, shaking his head.

"Of course it is, son." Evan's father squeezed his shoulder. Then he stepped forward to address Sela directly. "I'm glad you're giving us this chance."

The man's betrayal was at the forefront of her mind, but she read sincerity in his eyes. Was she too naive to judge a man's character? Or at least this man's?

"All right, Dad." Evan grabbed his father's arm and ushered him out. "Let me have a word with her alone."

Evan's father didn't seem like the kind of man who would be herded anywhere, but then she saw him smile again. Evan shut the door behind him then approached Sela and shoved his hands on his hips.

His nearness sent her mind reeling. His lips slowly spread into a smile.

Not sure about her reasons for coming. Not sure at all.

She'd done it now, involving herself with his father personally.

Evan pushed his fury down. For now. As he gazed into Sela's searching stormy-ocean eyes, the way they shimmered with hope, how could Evan do anything else but smile in return? Besides, this wasn't her fault. How did he make her understand that she should leave now and never look back?

Too late for that. His father would never let go until he had what he wanted, one way or another. Evan sighed.

He'd planned to speak with his father today about transferring back to the Virginia Beach office, which would mean giving up his promotion. But he wasn't on board with this development project near the Smith River, after everything that had happened.

He'd been torn about whether to stay or not. His father's behavior bordered on unethical, and his betrayal in not telling Evan about his brother was difficult to let go.

No matter what, Evan loved his father. But he needed some space from the man so he could think things through clearly without being influenced. His desire for approval battled with the respect he was quickly losing for his own father. Leaving would be the best thing for now, putting distance between him and Sela, too. She consumed his thoughts—but she was tied up in the clash with his father.

On the other hand, he needed to stay here and work on this project so he could find out why his father wanted that property. Evan would need to be here to stand in his way. He would need to be here to protect Sela.

He sighed, knowing that she had just made the decision for him.

She didn't understand that Robert Black would play on her sympathies and desires to reach out to David's family. Evan hated admitting it, but he was beginning to see his father in a new light. In a way he'd failed to see before. Either Evan had ignored the truth or he'd not previously been subjected to a situation that brought out the darker motives driving his father.

In the end, Evan feared that the man would use and abuse Sela in every way possible. Acid burned in his gut. He hoped he was wrong.

Sela looked away, probably reacting to his expression. He'd been silent, caught up in tumultuous thoughts that had turned his smile to a frown.

Evan couldn't stand to see the hurt in her eyes. He couldn't stand to cause her pain for another millisecond. "I can't believe you're here after everything," he said. "Why would you want anything to do with me or my father?"

"I told you already. And...I can't simply forget that David's brother and father are within a few miles of me. I'd like to get to know you better."

Again, Evan shook his head. "My father wants that property, Sela. I don't know why it's so important to him. I'm afraid he'll persuade you into doing something you shouldn't."

"Give me some credit. I'm not young and naive." She tucked a strand of her gorgeous auburn locks behind her ear, looking so much younger than she was. Sela was regal and sophisticated. But she was wrong—she was, in fact, innocent and naive. How could all of those qualities exist in one woman?

"My father didn't build this company without knowing how to persuade even the most experienced businessmen." Evan suddenly questioned what tactics his father had used in the past when faced with someone like Sela who refused to consider his propositions.

"Look, Evan. I'm starting to feel like an idiot for coming. It's just that you spoke with such finality, and it was too much to take given that we'd only just met. I finally met David's brother, his father—family he would have wanted to know. I thought maybe we could spend a little time together, that's all. Maybe you'd like to hear about your brother."

Evan pursed his lips. He wasn't sure that living in the past was what was best for Sela at all. A vibrant, beautiful woman like her should be living her life to the fullest. In fact, she should already be remarried by now. He figured she hadn't allowed anyone to get that close.

Yet she'd admitted to him that she liked him. There could have been something more between them...until this.

He stifled his despondent sigh and offered a slight smile. "I'd like that. But let's keep this between us, okay? No need to involve my father more than necessary."

Sela rewarded him with her beautiful, affectionate smile. "Agreed. This is good. Maybe we can try to put aside what happened. Start over. I'm sure David would want this."

What about you, Sela? What do you want? Sela appeared to try so hard to move beyond everything. Evan didn't have it in him to deny her. "Thank you for the painting, by the way. It means a lot to me."

"It was my pleasure." She pulled her gaze from him to look at the painting. "I have the tools in my Suburban and can hang it for you, if you'd like. I had already planned to do that, actually."

Glancing at his watch, Evan frowned. "I have a conference call here in fifteen minutes. I'll do it later."

He searched her eyes. Did she guess the reasons he'd initially wanted to purchase it? Those reasons now left him unsettled.

"Well, then, I guess I should get going." She tugged her keys from the pocket of her formfitting jeans and glanced at the floor then back up to him, bashful like a schoolgirl.

Sophisticated. Young. All in one package.

"Leave me your cell number, and I'll call you next week," he said. "We'll hang out, and you can tell me all about the brother I never knew."

Her smile faltered. Was this more for her than she was letting on? Evan found himself hoping that was the case. She grabbed a scrap of paper and a pen from his desk and scribbled on it.

"Looking forward to hearing from you." She smiled then exited his office, leaving her citrus perfume to envelop him.

Leaving him to wonder if it had all been a dream.

Could something more grow between them in the face of all that stood in the way? Did Evan want it to? Was he being manipulative by not telling her if he did? He'd forgotten how complicated a relationship could be.

Without even trying, Sela had all but shoved aside his decision to avoid getting involved again. But then again, they were just getting together so she could share memories of his brother with him. Whatever it was that he had with her was more complicated than anything he'd experienced before.

And the fallout would likely be more painful.

Sophisticated and young. Naive and wise—opposing qualities wrapped up in one person.

Evan figured that only Sela could bring with her both hope and dread. Evan's heart thrilled at the possibility of a future with her, and yet he was also terrified at a possible, devastating heartbreak. Still, she was worth it.

And regardless of what happened between them, Evan would protect her from his father's machinations.

He stared out the window in time to see his father traipse off toward the pier. What was that about? Evan was too distracted for the conference call now and decided to reschedule. He had a few words to give his father.

Well-chosen but respectful words.

Chapter 8

Evan trekked through the tall grass toward the beach and pier. The salty ocean breeze replaced the scent of Sela's perfume that clung to him.

His father rarely left his office during work hours except for business appointments. But then again, Evan hadn't spent much time on the West Coast until recently, so maybe this was his father's habit—a way to get some fresh air and clear his head.

Hands in the pockets of his tan slacks, Evan walked across the wooden slats that formed the pier, a forceful breeze pressing against him. His father stood at the end of the pier, leaning against the railing and staring out over the vast ocean. Something he could have done in his office sans the wind.

Evan rested against the railing next to him. "You come out here often?"

His father didn't acknowledge Evan's presence but continued to stare into the distance. "It helps to remember things sometimes," he finally said.

"Remember what?"

"Things that happened long before you were born." The man's tone had turned somber. He didn't even sound like Evan's always-in-control father.

Maybe Sela's appearance today had reminded him of the son he'd not had time with. Evan almost regretted the conversation he'd come here to have. But not completely. "What things?"

"Is there a reason you came all the way out here, Evan?"

So he wasn't prepared to share the memories. "Actually, yes."

"Thought so." His father turned to face him now, the breeze kicking up a notch so that he had to squint a little. "I'm proud of you, son. You made a lot more progress with Sela than I'd thought, if, after everything, she still wants to see you."

The anger he'd buried inside exploded. "Did you say that thinking you'd stir something up?"

His father smiled. "Not at all, but apparently I have anyway. Must have hit a chord of truth."

"What is wrong with you?" Evan shoved from the railing to leave his father standing there. But no, wait. He had a few things to say. He returned, biting back the bitterness in his tone. "Sela isn't interested in me like that. You heard why she showed up. She wants to know David's family."

"And you believe that?"

"Of course I do. Why wouldn't I?" With those words Evan knew he was lying to himself. His father saw through that. Evan was suddenly afraid he was just like his father. *Please, no.*

Ocean waves crashed against the pier and nearby rocky

outcroppings. Evan felt like a broken vessel being tossed to and fro. Slammed against the rocks.

His father exhaled long and slow. Also uncharacteristic of him. "Whatever the reason, we're fortunate she's interested in a little family time."

That's just what I thought you'd say. "You should know up front that I won't stand idly by and watch you wear her down." When his father didn't respond, Evan sucked in a sharp breath and forged ahead. "Please tell me you aren't interested in Sela's property anymore. You don't need it. This whole thing is insane."

"All right, I won't tell you I'm interested."

But Evan heard the sarcasm in his words. "You will never have that property. It belongs to her."

"Then you will never be part of the management team."

So be it. "If you could just tell me why you want it. It's just three hundred acres in your vast kingdom. Why, Dad?"

Brows drawn together, his father stepped away from the railing. "All in good time, son, all in good time."

Then he left Evan to stand there alone with more questions than answers. In his father's presence he felt like a troubled teenager again. Angry. Conflicted. If it weren't for those two emotions, he'd be completely empty. He wasn't sure which state of mind was worse.

Evan watched his father walk the length of the pier and grow smaller in the distance as he made his way back to the bank building. It was then Evan noticed the old fisherman who sat a few yards away—within earshot. The same fisherman, if he remembered correctly, he'd seen the last time he'd come out here, and every one of the few times he'd walked the pier. Somehow the man was so much a part of the scenery—like a fixture, a part of the railing—that he'd become invisible. Evan hadn't taken much notice until that moment.

The fisherman must have sensed Evan watching because he looked up then, and his eyes locked with Evan's. His face wrinkled and weathered like someone who spent years at sea, he smiled. Evan found himself drawn to the man and strolled his way. He leaned against the rail, thinking to strike up a conversation. Find out how much the man overheard. Not that it really mattered.

But something in this man's eyes made Evan curious to know more. "You come here often?" Evan cringed, remembering he'd asked his father the exact same question. Some conversationalist he was.

The fisherman chuckled, sounding old and raspy, warmth suffusing his laugh. "Yes, but not for the memories, for the fish."

"I see," Evan said. So the man had heard their conversation. With the wind whipping around, Evan wasn't certain. "The fishing is good here, then."

"Silver salmon, king salmon, lingcod, red snapper, black snapper, sea bass, steelhead. You name it, I've caught it. Some days are better than others. Used to have a boat. Used to have a father, too."

Evan was the one to laugh this time. "Yep. Everyone needs a father. That's unfortunate sometimes."

"That's the truth. A bad father can distort our image of our heavenly Father God."

The words stunned Evan. You never knew what to expect when talking to strangers. "I suppose that could be true." Though he really didn't know God well enough to say.

"No supposing to it; it's the truth. Spend enough time with the Lord and you'll find out, son. I suspect your father needs time with the Almighty as well. God is good to us. He's the giver of all good gifts. Only He can fill those holes in your heart left by your earthly father."

There was no arguing that Evan had put expectations on his father—maybe he shouldn't have. He definitely had a lot of holes, or wounds, brought on by those expectations not being fulfilled. Here Evan was trying to please the man, hoping he'd tell Evan how proud he was of him, when Evan couldn't say he was proud in return—at least not in the face of his father's recent actions surrounding David, Sela, and the three hundred acres.

Could God—a deeper relationship with Him—fill the emptiness and wash Evan's anger and resentment away? Was that what was missing in his life? Evan hung his head, the truth infusing every crack in his soul.

"But how does He fill the holes? How can He?" Why was he asking this poor fisherman, a complete stranger? How could he know anything about it? Yet somehow… Evan knew the man had an answer.

"Spend time with Him and you'll find out." The old fisherman pulled in his fishing line and fiddled with the bait. "There's no time like the present. Every day is a new day with God."

Sela's words came back to him: *"Maybe we can try to put aside what happened. Start over."* Could Evan really do that? Let go of his resentment toward his father? Apparently, there was a way to find out.

Evan believed in God and His Son, but he admitted, he hadn't exactly allowed God to be a real part of his life.

There was no time like the present.

Sela stood on the deck of the *Golden Eagle*—the forty-four-foot fishing boat that Evan had chartered.

She'd been more than wary about coming today, but considering that getting together to share memories of David with Evan had been her idea, she hadn't had the heart to say no. She might have suggested something else, but Evan had already chartered a boat. He hadn't known, of course, how David died. What an awkward situation.

On the other hand, something inside told her that she needed to do this, to go boating—that being here was part of the healing process, part of the closure.

But it was difficult—memories of the times they'd spent on David's boat accosted her. Still, the images weren't as vivid as she would have thought. Instead they were blurry, as if fading into the distance. She had to admit that being near Evan was part of the reason. Even now he yanked her thoughts from the past.

Despite the cap she wore to keep her hair in place, wind whipped a strand over her face when she turned to watch Evan and his friend fishing. Evan's fishing pole suddenly jerked, drawing Sela's full attention. What had he hooked?

"Keep reelin'. Keep reelin'," Tom said. The older fisherman's eyes brightened, and he quickly lost his hunched-over look. He eased closer to Evan but continued to hold his own rod and reel.

Evan's rod arced over. "Whatever it is, it has to be big."

"Nah, he's just fighting you." Tom's enthusiasm transformed him into a much younger man.

"That's what I'm afraid of," Evan yelled.

"Don't let him best you." Tom's expression animated, he appeared to enjoy Evan's experience as if it were his own.

The old fisherman instructed Evan as he reeled in his catch of the day. After an exhilarating battle, Evan finally drew the fish closer, where it flopped around against the boat amid hoots and hollers. Tom reached over the side with a gaff and snagged the fish.

Evan assisted Tom in tugging it onto the boat. The huge, ugly creature had teeth like a shark and continued to struggle.

"What *is* that?" Evan asked, both his brows arched high.

Sela laughed. "It's a lingcod—ugly and prehistoric looking, isn't it?"

"I thought I was trying to catch a salmon. Should we throw it back?" Evan looked to Tom for an answer.

Tom's grin covered his face. "This makes great fish chowder and will last a long time. I'll cook up a big batch. You can tell me what you think."

"That's a deal," Evan said, although he didn't look that sure.

He assisted Tom in carrying the lingcod to the live well on the boat. "You've been fishing your whole life?"

"I come from a long line of Portuguese fishermen, whalers mostly, that worked off the California coast." Tom's voice faded with the wind as they made their way around the boat in the opposite direction.

Sela left the men to it and went to stand at the bow, wondering why she'd been invited along in the first place. She sensed that Tom was good for Evan, and that made her smile. Although she could have fished along with them, just being on the boat was enough for her today.

She leaned her head back, hoping the sun would warm her face in spite of the cold bite of the wind. She'd spent some time in Southern California, and the difference in the warmer water and beaches always astounded her.

With her back to the rest of the boat, she stared out over the Pacific.

"I have a feeling I'd be one of those people who would get seasick if the water was even a little choppy." Evan's voice surprised her. She hadn't heard his approach.

He seemed relaxed. Happy.

"I wouldn't have wanted to come, either, if the forecast hadn't been perfect." She gazed at him and smiled, though he couldn't have known her struggle over joining him in the first place, unless he'd done some research. But she was certain he hadn't, considering the reason he gave for the fishing trip. "I can't tell you how surprised I was when you called to invite me deep-sea fishing."

"I wanted to do this for a new friend, and I thought you might enjoy coming along."

"Is Tom still fishing?"

"Yeah, but I'm done. Besides, I didn't plan to spend the whole time fishing or else I wouldn't have invited you."

When he called, Evan explained that he'd recently met someone on the pier near the Blackwood offices and that Tom had offered words of wisdom that Evan had taken to heart. The fact that Evan had wanted to take him deep-sea fishing to return the kindness touched Sela like a finger stirring the waters of her soul. The kind of person who'd do that was rare these days.

"I'm surprised my father didn't want to come. He overheard me chartering the boat, and I expected him to invite himself along. But he made it clear he wasn't a fan of boating or fishing."

"Hmm. I wonder why."

"I don't know. That must explain why he doesn't have his own boat. I'd expect him to have one just to entertain others, impress them."

"What about you? It looked like you weren't that experienced."

Evan laughed. "That obvious, huh? This was my first time to fish."

"Your father never took you as a kid?"

"Nope. He was a workaholic and still is. I didn't have much time with him. And my mother died about ten years ago. She was the one who insisted on all those classical guitar lessons."

"I'm sorry to hear that about your mother," Sela said. "Mine died from cancer. David and I were already married. Six months later his mother died—she'd been struggling with leukemia. I guess that's why David wanted to live with her after we were married."

"I bet that made for an interesting experience."

"I won't deny it was a challenge as newlyweds. She was a bit eccentric. Paranoid, even." Sela shoved her errant hair away along with the more unpleasant memories of that time.

"Paranoid? Maybe that explains the pistol I found stored in that desk I bought. It was old, hadn't been cleaned. I'd forgotten about it until now."

Sela chuckled. "Yes. Had to be hers. I found weapons—knives and one small pistol—hidden or stored in the oddest places. I thought she was just losing her mind. That her illness had somehow brought on the paranoia and fear that someone was after her. I've heard that happens sometimes."

"Really."

Sela rubbed her ring finger, now devoid of a wedding ring. "I didn't have the heart to make too much out of it to David. I mean, it was clear she wouldn't last much longer. I just wanted to be a good wife."

Then after his mother was gone, Sela couldn't bring herself to press him about changing the decor and furnishings—after all, he'd lost his mother. She could give him time to grieve.

"How about *your* mother?" she asked.

"Car accident, and I was an only child—"

The words appeared to hit him the same time they hit Sela. His smile faltered, and his gaze drifted to a dark place in the distance. *But you had a half brother....*

"I've met your sister Alexa, but not Camille, the artist whose painting I bought."

"You knew the artist was my sister?"

"The lady at your shop told me." Evan grinned. Sela liked that his smile was back, replacing the look of distant, unwelcome memories in his eyes.

"Camille lives in Redbrook with her husband, who runs an Italian restaurant. She's seriously talented, just like Alexa." Sela sighed, feeling once again like the talent she had, if any, had been tied up in David's creations, his guitars.

"And your father?" Evan asked.

"He left when we were kids." Now *that* was a story Sela didn't feel like reminiscing. Alexa had spent her childhood and part of adulthood believing that she was the reason their parents had split. That getting lost in the redwoods had led to their parents' fighting and their father eventually leaving. But Sela knew their parents' problems went much deeper. Best to change the subject now, though, and move to remembering David. That was the purpose of their time together, wasn't it?

But where did she start? In the distance, she spotted a lighthouse. She'd always wanted to take a tour, but David never did. Sela pointed to the northeast. "From here, you can just make out St. George Reef Lighthouse. See it?"

Evan squinted, staring in the direction she pointed. "It's quite a ways from the coast."

"It was built as a direct result of the *Brother Jonathan* shipwreck on the Dragon Rocks—a cluster of rocks and outcroppings about seven miles from the coast. I've always wanted to visit there."

He looked her way, studying her. "You want me to have the *Golden Eagle* take us?"

"Oh, no. It's run by a historical society now, and you have to schedule a tour that takes you there by helicopter."

"That could be fun." He grinned. "Living so close to

the coast, did you and David ever go boating? Or deep-sea fishing?"

"Yes. David and I used to go boating. He'd fish, and I'd watch for whales. But…he died in a boating accident. Drowned." Sela hung her head, recalling the day she'd learned the news. Surprisingly, thinking on it now was less painful than she would have thought.

"Oh, Sela. I'm sorry." Evan squeezed the railing, his knuckles white. "I didn't know. I should have asked you how he died or at least done my own research. Inviting you today was insensitive of me. But learning that I had a half brother was hard enough. I guess I wasn't ready to hear more. It was just too much too fast."

The distress in his voice told her he was berating himself. She touched his arm. "It's all right. I'm glad you invited me. I was worried about how I would feel, being on a boat again. But the accident in which he died happened almost five years ago."

"That explains your initial reaction. When I called, I thought you were having second thoughts about us getting together." He gazed at her then, his eyes gently probing. "Were you with him that day?"

"No." She tore her gaze away and watched the ocean instead, hoping to see a whale. Orcas, especially, were often seen here, looking for salmon just like the fishermen. "I was visiting Aunt Erin and Camille in Redbrook. Storms can come in swiftly, turning the ocean ugly. He should have known better. I don't know why he went out alone that day. Who knows if it would have made any difference had someone else been along?"

"I hope it doesn't upset you to talk about it. I shouldn't have asked. Let's talk about happier times."

A small laughed escaped. "It's not as difficult to talk about as I thought it would be. That's why we're here together, isn't it? To talk about David. Maybe next time you should come to my home, and I'll show you pictures."

But she wasn't sure that's what she wanted, either—to show Evan pictures of his brother, her deceased husband. She wanted to climb from this hole she'd hidden in, to move on.

She released a long exhale. Finally...finally, she had the desire to press forward. To move on. She couldn't help but think Evan was the reason.

What was happening? The painful memories that she'd clung to for so long—far too long—weren't nearly as painful anymore. She'd thought being with Evan would help her feel connected to David and in a way would honor his memory. Standing next to Evan—his good looks, kind heart, and masculinity—the fog over her heart and mind slowly lifted. And with the lifting, she saw more clearly now that her desperate need to hold on to the past was unhealthy at best.

Evan watched her. She smiled, hoping to cover the sudden melancholy that had nothing at all to do with Evan.

"I'd like to see photographs of my brother. Sure, we can do that, too. But I'll be honest with you, I'm still struggling with finding out that I had a brother and now he's gone." Evan's voice cracked, revealing the weight of his emotions.

"Have you talked this through with your father? Or are you holding it all in?"

"You mean am I holding in my resentment and bitterness at his duplicity?" Evan offered an incredulous laugh. "I don't want to throw in a sour note on a pleasant afternoon. So, I'll just say this: Tom has helped me see that I have to turn to God for answers."

Sela's heart caught in her throat. She slipped her hand over Evan's, and he gazed down at her touch, his eyes tender. "I'm so glad to hear that, Evan. There isn't anyone else who can help you more than God. All we can do is pray for your father, but first we have to forgive him."

"Really? You've forgiven him already?"

"Like you, I'm trusting God to help me with that. But I learned a long time ago I can't change people, and it's not my place to judge them. It's my place to love people and pray for them. Let God do the rest."

Evan didn't respond but looked out at the clouds brewing in the distance, threatening the calm waters.

"If I've said too much, I'm sorry," she said. "It's none of my business what happens between you and your father."

He studied her with great intensity, but she fought the need to look away. "I can see what my brother saw in you—you're not only strikingly beautiful on the outside, but your beauty runs all the way through."

Heat rushed through her insides and caressed her cheeks. Hearing such words from Evan—a man she now knew to be David's brother—sounded strange and should have been uncomfortable.

But his words pleased her, made her heart breach the waters.

Chapter 9

A week had passed since she'd been boating with Evan, but it felt like much longer. Her first time on the ocean since David's death, the day on the *Golden Eagle*, was an important step forward for her, and Evan had made the difference.

She'd shared with him her memories of David well after the boat had docked at the marina and they'd said goodbye to Tom, making plans to get together for a bowl of his lingcod fish chowder. She couldn't stop thinking about that day. Or about Evan.

When she received a request for a custom guitar, she hesitated but decided that would keep her busy in the evenings, taking her mind off Evan and his sudden but complicated appearance in her life.

But it hadn't worked like she had hoped. She found herself making mistakes that David would never have made. Add to that, the guitar reminded her of the day Evan had played for her, serenading her with classical guitar music—his talent equal to David's, if not greater. She would never look at a guitar again without remembering that day—the day she and Evan discovered the truth.

Her idea to take on this project to occupy her mind had backfired, in a sense. So had her plan to honor David's memory by sharing memories of him with his brother. Her interest in Evan, her desire to spend time with him, had nothing to do with David and everything to do with Evan. She'd fooled herself into thinking otherwise.

Running her hand over the piece of rosewood she would use for the tone wood, she sighed—she wanted to hear Evan play again, and…she missed him. The fact that he was on the other side of the country this week working in the Virginia Beach office didn't help. He'd gone there to personally oversee complications with a property he'd managed. She hoped the problem would be resolved quickly. Maybe the distance had put a sharp edge to her need to see him, to hear his voice.

Her cell rang, and she snatched it up. Her heart pounded. Was it Evan? The caller ID told her it was. A smile ignited in her heart, spreading to her lips. She was in junior high again. *Pathetic.* "Evan, hi. It's good to hear from you."

"I hope I'm not interrupting anything."

"Not at all. I'm working on a commissioned guitar. I can see now that it was a mistake to take on the project. I don't know what I was thinking." *Yes, I do. I was thinking about you.*

"I'll be back in town on Friday evening. I wondered if Saturday would be all right for me to come over. You could show me those pictures of David. Tell me more stories about him."

Her shoulders sagged. Was that the only reason he wanted to see her? Or was he using that as an excuse? Or both? Was she setting herself up to be hurt? There might be a way to find out. She hesitated, unsure if she was doing the right thing. "Listen…"

"Sela, if you don't—"

"Let me finish," she said. She'd caught the disappointment in his tone. He thought she was turning his invitation down, but that wasn't it at all. "I've been cooped up working in the gift shop every day and in the room David set up as his guitar shop in the evenings. Would you mind if we had a picnic, or walked the beach? I need to get out of the house." *I could bring photo albums if you'd like.* She thought it but didn't say it.

Silence met her on the line. What was he thinking? Desperation shot through her. "We can talk about David, too, if you want…." Sela squeezed her eyes shut, her heart racing. "Or not. Evan, we don't have to talk about David." There. She'd said it. Would he understand her meaning?

"I've missed you this week, Sela."

His voice made her want to crawl through the phone line. "I've missed you, too."

"But I thought the only reason you wanted to be with me was to share memories of David," he said.

Sela opened her mouth to speak.

"But a walk on the beach with you would be nice. I'd like that very much. I liked being with you before I knew about my brother. You know that. I'm concerned about—"

"Your father. My land. I know. But I think we're past that now, don't you?"

"I'm not convinced."

Sela sighed. *Not this again.*

"I'll stop by Saturday morning around nine. If we're lucky, maybe we'll catch a decent low tide. I've always wanted to see a tide pool but haven't had the chance yet."

The things this man has never done. "I love to go tidepooling. I have plenty of pictures to show you, but the real thing is much better."

"Yes, I imagine looking at a living, breathing starfish would be better than looking at a snapshot."

This had been a good day. He wished it didn't have to end.

A big wave washed up the beach nearly reaching Sela's bare toes, though she and Evan were hundreds of feet from the water's edge. Evan straddled a driftwood log, bleached out from the sun, while Sela sat in the sand, leaning against the log.

They had spent the last few Saturdays on the beach now, and Evan still hadn't caught a low tide so he could look at starfish and sea anemones in the tide pools. The next low tide was due to hit at 4:00 a.m. on Tuesday. That was so not happening. But this—spending time with Sela like this—he could get used to. He didn't care if he ever saw a tide pool.

She was the most genuine person that Evan had ever known, and he savored these times with her.

"I think the tide is coming in more. You ready to head back?" He slid from the log, landing next to Sela and spraying her with sand.

"Hey, watch it," she said, laughing.

"Oh, come on. You can't come to the beach and not expect to get a little sand on you." Evan offered his hand. *You can't spend time with Sela and not expect to fall for her.* The thought made him wince inside. He'd walked into this with his eyes wide open.

When she placed her hand in his, he assisted her up, her slim frame barely requiring any effort on his part. When she was on her feet, he released her hand, though he really wanted to hold it as they walked.

He had the urge to grip her waist and lift her high in the air, swinging her around. But no. He didn't want to press her. Urging her into something more before he knew for certain she wanted it wouldn't do either of them any good.

But that was just it. He believed she did want more between them. Evan just didn't know what to do about it. His relationships with his father and Sela had become so convoluted.

They strolled along the beach, heading back toward where he'd parked, though the walk was still quite a distance. That was all part of the plan—the farther they walked, the more time he could spend with her.

He frowned, again wondering if he was being manipulative. Conniving like his father. He hoped not. And yet, how could he really be sure?

A person may think their own ways are right, but the Lord weighs the heart.

The verse in Proverbs leaped from his heart like it had become a living, breathing part of him. He'd been reading his Bible lately, trying to learn more about God. Getting to know Him better. *Lord, please help me to do the right thing by Sela. Help me to see if I'm with her for the wrong reasons.*

It felt good to have Someone to talk to. And good to be with Sela.

Sure, he was skirting around the fact that he cared deeply for her—more than as a simple friend or as the wife of his deceased brother. The way she looked at him, reacted to him, he was certain she felt the same.

Still, they danced around David.

Not only had they spent Saturdays together, they'd attended church together a couple of Sundays in a row now. But after service she'd had to work on the guitar project she'd taken, which was fine because Evan had plenty of his own work on the Smith River development project to do—minus Sela's three hundred acres.

Busy with his own demands, his father ended up keeping him on the project without much interference. Evan didn't doubt that was because his father believed he was deep in the process of persuading Sela to sell. The man had deluded himself, and Evan had left things at that.

Let him believe what he wanted. Evan knew it would do no good to bring up the subject of Sela's land with his father because it would only lead to the same argument again. Instead, he hoped to exceed the man's expectations for the luxury housing community *without* Sela's property. She'd tried to discuss her property with Evan a time or two, but he refused—the last thing he wanted was for her to think he spent time with her to get to her property. If everything worked according to his plans, then Sela would keep her land, his father's demands would be met, and Evan would still earn his promotion.

Everyone would be happy.

As far as his inner turmoil regarding his father, he tried to work through his problems with prayer.

Strolling next to him, Sela released a contented sigh, bringing his thoughts back to her, though they'd never gone too far away.

In addition to spending a good part of the weekend together, they talked on the phone a few times a week, growing closer. All under the guise of getting to know each other for the sake of a dead man whose troubles were over.

The night he'd called her from Virginia Beach, he'd missed her in a deep, aching way. And based on their conversation, he thought she'd been ready to push beyond David—she'd said as much, stating they didn't *have* to talk about David the next time they got together. Evan had taken that to mean she wanted to spend time with him because she liked him.

But then, she'd brought out the photo albums, effectively putting David between them again. Evan enjoyed hearing more about him, but he didn't like the way his brother continued to stand between them. How did he push his relationship with Sela past this, especially when he believed that Sela wanted to move on? That it wasn't just something *he* wanted?

His attraction to her went far behind the physical and had never changed, even after hearing about his brother. He was drawn to her in spite of everything that had happened.

"What are you thinking?" she asked, strolling next to him.

Evan stopped and turned to face her. How would she react if he told her what he was *really* thinking?

The breeze had let up a little, but still her auburn hair escaped the clip she always wore at the beach and whipped across her face, her lips.

He reached up to pull the strands away. When his finger touched her lips, he allowed it to linger there. A deep ache coursed through him. She shut her eyes as if savoring his touch.

Evans's mouth went dry. He longed to kiss her, to press his lips against hers, feel her warmth and tenderness, her passion. He edged closer, but then she abruptly opened her eyes and pulled the hair from her face, refastening it behind her head.

What just happened?

Though their almost intimate moment had ended, he saw longing in her eyes. And that nearly undid him. Her reaction was the nudge he needed to take the next step. But for the first time since their unusual relationship had started, it occurred to Evan that Sela could be using him—in a way—to replace David or be David for her.

Oh, I hope not. With the thought, his lungs seemed to deflate completely. Why hadn't he considered this before?

Evan took a step closer. "Sela," he whispered, "I need you to understand that I'm not my brother."

"I know." The way she said the words spoke to his heart, though her simple, soft smile would have been enough. In her eyes he saw what he wanted to see.

A barking dog ran between them, separating them, followed by one, two, then three laughing children. Evan and Sela laughed, too. The moment to kiss her was lost but not forever.

She was a treasure to him, buried deep in the redwoods. More than anything he feared that someone, namely, his father, would persist in efforts to dig up the treasure, to steal everything away.

Chapter 10

After a day at the beach, Evan treated Sela to dinner at a seafood restaurant. Before entering, she scraped the sand off the best she could and hoped that no one paid much attention to the two sandy beachcombers.

Chances were, she and Evan weren't the only ones who'd come directly from the beach looking to slake their appetite with lobster or smoked salmon.

Evan was a delight to be with, and time with him passed much too quickly for her. As he drove her home, she enjoyed the comfortable silence between them. Likely, he was thinking about their day, and she hoped he enjoyed it as much as she had.

"I'm not my brother."

Ever since he'd first spoken the words, they'd twirled in her mind, her heart. Even with the little things he'd done that reminded her of David, she'd never for an instant thought of Evan as anyone other than himself. She hoped he knew that. And for a moment, after he'd touched her lips and said the words, she thought he might kiss her.

But she'd been scared and brushed the moment away. What was the matter with her?

She watched the headlights of cars passing in the night, surprised at how much she'd wanted that kiss in hindsight. She'd started this—whatever it was—to get to know David's family. At least that's what she told herself. But she hadn't been completely honest. She'd hidden that truth away, fearing if she discovered it, she would run. But it was too late to run.

Nor did Sela want to.

Evan turned into the driveway and pulled beyond the gift shop to her home, shrouded in darkness. The security light was out, but thank goodness she'd thought to leave the porch light on when she'd left with him this morning.

By the time she'd slung her purse over her shoulder and gathered her beach bag and blanket—items they hadn't used today—Evan had opened the door for her. More often lately, she felt like their friendly excursions were dates.

"Here, let me help you carry some of that," Evan said and took the towel and her beach bag.

Evan was the only man other than David that she'd allowed this close to her. She'd dated David all through high school—even though he'd been a little older than her, in his early twenties then, it felt like they had been high school sweethearts—so it wasn't like there had been much opportunity for her to date other men. Losing David was like losing herself, or at least a part of herself. Mending had been difficult and slow, and she hadn't had the energy or the desire to move past the pain.

Until recently. Until Evan.

As they crunched across the gravelly, dimly lit drive, Sela realized she still feared trusting him. She'd been the one to pursue the relationship, and she wanted to trust him with everything in her. But a niggling of doubt remained that perhaps he'd wormed his way into her life, after all. That he'd used his charm to exploit her loneliness.

Yet, he'd come to mean everything to her. How could she feel this way about a man she didn't trust completely?

Maybe she was naive after all, unable to judge a man's character. She'd been unable to read his father. What if Evan, like his father, was after her land? And why, after several weeks, was she suddenly bombarded with these doubts?

Lost in fear and dread, Sela hadn't realized she'd stopped walking until she noticed Evan staring at her.

"What's wrong?" he asked. He took the remainder of her things from her and set them on an ornate bench encircling a tree near the porch. "Sela, are you all right?"

Had spending time with him been a grave mistake fueled by her desperate loneliness?

"Sela?" He took her hands in his and rubbed them, warming the chill out of them.

"I'm sorry…. I just… I'm scared."

Even in what light illuminated his face, sympathy flooded his eyes. "I hope you're not scared of me. Of us," he said. Desperation flooded his voice.

She'd only ever loved one man, trusted one man. When Evan had shown up on her doorstep, she'd found herself willing to consider opening her heart to someone else, but all the drama surrounding their lives was still there.

"I don't want to be. Help me, Evan."

"I'm scared, too, but I'm sure that's not what you want to hear. I don't have ulterior motives here, Sela. It's not my intention to hurt you. If it makes you feel any better, my heart is at risk of being hurt, too. I'll do my best to make sure that doesn't happen to either of us." His steadfast gaze reassured her.

She believed he meant every word.

He lifted a strand of her hair then released the rest of her mane from the clip, weaving his hands through. Other than today, when he'd briefly touched her lips, he'd never touched her or reached for her in a romantic way in the time they'd spent together. Always simply a friend, a gentleman, despite the current of attraction between them— the one she'd tried to ignore for so long now.

But no longer.

Evan moved his hand from her hair to her cheek, running his thumb around the curve of her jaw. Pleasant warmth enveloped her, and her chest rose and fell with the sensations coursing through her. Sensations brought on by one effortless touch from this man.

Evan stepped closer, his face mere inches from hers. He took his time, gazing into her eyes.

"I'm not my brother."

No. He wasn't his brother. Sela shut her eyes, wanting, expecting what Evan would do next.

His breath feathered her cheeks before his lips found hers. Gentle. Soft. Exploring the contours of her lips. She could sense the eagerness behind his kiss, yet he held back, constraining the longing that connected them both now through a simple touch.

A kiss.

A meeting of hearts that was everything it should be.

The kiss stirred her beyond the physical, flowing deep into her soul, it seemed. Evan didn't press further, didn't wrap her in his arms, but held back. She loved that he was a patient man. He allowed his lips to linger against hers. Then he eased away, remaining close, his peppermint breath fanning her cheeks.

"I hope I haven't overstepped." A husky tone crept into his voice.

"I hope we can do this again." Her own voice sounded strange. Distant somehow. Drifting on her affection for Evan.

Evan laughed softly and pressed his forehead against hers. "I think I can arrange that."

"I'm looking forward to it." Sela smiled.

When Evan stepped back, his eyes were gentle, as though he was still lost in the pleasure, the experience of their shared kiss. He smiled. "It's getting late. I'd better get you inside."

Sela floated to her front door and unlocked it, Evan by her side, carrying her things. It had been so long since she'd been this happy, she could hardly contain herself. She shoved the door open and flipped on the lights.

Her bookshelf lay on the floor, books scattered everywhere. The love seat was turned over and sliced open, the padding ripped out.

Evan watched the deputy's patrol car pull from Sela's drive.

After he shut the door, he found Sela rubbing her arms as if chilled, even though her home was warm. He hugged her to him, wanting to comfort and reassure her. She trembled against him. He hated that someone had done this to her home.

To her. To them. Slicing a piece out of what would have been a memorable evening and ruining the memory of their first kiss.

She edged out of his embrace and rubbed her eyes then glanced at him. Dark circles revealed her exhaustion. "I don't understand why anyone would do this."

"Remember what the deputy said. Property crimes—

theft and burglary—are the biggest problem in the county. But this county still has a low crime rate compared to the rest of the state."

Sela almost smiled. Almost.

"I know that doesn't do you any good. Do you want me to stay?" he asked. But when Sela's eyes grew wide, he quickly added, "I could sleep on the sofa, the one they hadn't gotten to yet, that is. That way you can sleep. You don't have to be afraid." He'd intended that from the start and hoped she didn't think poorly of him for the suggestion.

"You heard the man. They waited until I was gone, and they most likely won't return even though it appears they hadn't finished their search for valuables. It was a simple burglary, though I'm still not sure what they took. What they were looking for. What did they think was in my furniture anyway?" A deep frown creasing her forehead, she shook her head.

"At least they didn't find your guitars interesting." Evan gripped Sela's arms and peered into her lovely face, worn with the aftermath of a long day followed by the shock of discovering her home burglarized. "Are you sure you're going to be all right?"

She smiled brightly. Too brightly. Obviously, she wanted to reassure him. "Yes, Evan. I'm so tired I couldn't care less if someone breaks in again, but I don't think we need to worry. I'll make sure the security light gets fixed tomorrow."

"And get an alarm system installed. I'll help clean up tomorrow, but tonight you should get some rest." The deputy had explained the county was too understaffed and underfunded to dust for prints, especially for a simple house break-in. In fact, he'd almost laughed at Evan's question.

"I still plan to go to church in the morning. I'd appreciate your help, though, after that." She grinned shyly, finally displaying some of the old, pre-burglary Sela—the woman he'd kissed only moments ago, before she'd unlocked and opened the door to chaos.

He read in her eyes that she wanted a sampling of what she'd experienced earlier, despite her home having been broken into. Evan was only too happy to oblige. He'd waited long enough for their relationship to take the next step. He hadn't been sure if it would or not, given the extenuating circumstances surrounding them.

"Come here," he said, his whisper guttural.

Sela stepped willingly into his arms and lifted her face, her lips, to meet his. He wouldn't press her any further than he'd done during their first kiss. He'd take things slow with her, savoring every step of their budding relationship.

That she was fragile, easily broken, he had no doubt. His need to protect her stirred inside. When he ended the brief kiss, she sighed against him, and he languished in the feel of her in his arms.

"Evan?" she asked softly.

"Hmm?" He caressed her back, hoping to coax away her remaining anxiety.

She leaned away from him, her gaze roaming his face then stopping at his eyes. "I wanted to make sure you knew—and we don't ever have to bring this up again—but I'm over David. And I never...for even one minute... thought of you as anyone but who you are."

The words he'd spoken to her that afternoon drifted back to him. He'd wanted to believe her earlier, the *first* time she'd answered him, ignoring the doubt that edged his thoughts.

"I believe you." He grinned then released her completely. "I'd better leave, or I'll end up standing here with you all night."

"Good night, Evan." Sela's sleepy smile twisted his heart, setting in concrete his hope for a future with her.

Evan backed his Tahoe into the shadows across the street. He considered that sitting in Sela's drive for all to see might be more of a deterrent to any would-be burglars, should they decide to return, but then she'd know he was there keeping vigil. She might wonder why he believed it necessary to stand watch, and he didn't want her to worry.

But the break-in disturbed him. A burglary was one thing—stealing valuables like electronics and jewelry, neither of which Sela owned in great quantity nor had been stolen—but the burglars had ripped into stuff in a frantic search. The two deputies had said as much but let the idea go when Sela had nothing to offer. The break-in potentially chalked up to another one in a rash of burglaries of late.

Evan adjusted his seat and settled in for a long, uncomfortable night. But he'd spent worse nights, and watching Sela's home gave him a measure of peace. For tonight.

Tomorrow was another day, and he'd take this one day at a time. He wouldn't be able to sleep at home anyway. In the stillness of the early morning hours, Evan waited and watched. He hoped he'd see nothing. His thoughts, meanwhile, sifted through the first day he'd met her and the reason why.

His father.

The man had worked for years to gain the necessary permits and rights from the state of California to develop the land surrounding Sela's acreage.

Robert Black's commanding voice resounded in Evan's head: *"Befriend her. Charm her. Whatever it takes.... Three hundred acres of prime real estate on the Smith River."*

Was Evan guilty of following through with his father's

devious wishes—though that had never been his intent—
if he found himself befriended, found himself charmed?
Found himself falling for her?

Chapter 11

"You're sure this is necessary?" Though she couldn't see a thing with the blindfold Evan had insisted on, she enjoyed the mystery. The only thing she knew for sure was that he'd driven her in circles for what felt like half an hour to confuse her.

"It's all part of the fun. It wouldn't be much of a surprise otherwise." He sounded like a schoolboy who'd just gotten a new puppy. "Wait right here, and I'll open the door for you. No peeking, either."

A thrill ran through her that he would put so much energy into this, whatever it was. That he wanted to surprise her. When she'd asked him what prompted the special occasion, he simply replied he wanted to take her on a real date, especially now that they were officially dating. She pressed him further, considering this was above and beyond what couples did on dates.

He'd replied that she was special enough, and they

didn't need a special occasion. But she suspected he was attempting to get her mind off the break-in.

His plan was working.

The Tahoe's door opened, pulling out of the firm grasp she'd kept on the handgrip, and Evan assisted her out. She heard the door shut, then he slipped his arm around her waist, holding her close as he led her across a hard surface. A prop plane powered up somewhere nearby. *The airport?*

"I can't stand it anymore. Where are you taking me?"

He chuckled. Sela loved his laugh and the resulting happiness that it sparked inside.

"I'm learning that you're not a very patient woman, Sela." He whispered in her ear. "Just a few more steps, and then…"

Evan lifted her into his arms. Sela yelped then giggled, enjoying it all too much. For a few seconds, he held her close. Cradling her gently, his breath was soft and warm against her face. Finally he relinquished her to a seat in another vehicle.

"No peeking." Evan kissed her cheek. "It's almost over."

Pressing her hand against her cheek where his lips had been, Sela smiled. From the other side, Evan slipped into a seat next to her. Doors closed around her.

"You ready?" a man's voice spoke from the front of whatever they were sitting in.

"Yes," Evan said.

"Can I take this off now?" Despite her initial excitement, impatience gnawed inside.

A whirring resonated, accompanied by a small vibration—*a helicopter?* A few moments later, her stomach flipped inside, leaving no doubt they had lifted off.

Evan slipped his hands around her head. *Thank goodness.*

When he removed the blindfold, he brandished a big,

sheepish grin. Sela glanced at her surroundings and gasped.

"I would have kept you guessing until we arrived at our destination, but I could see your patience was wearing thin." He grabbed her hand and brought it to his lips, pressing a gentle kiss there. Then he continued to hold her hand as the helicopter transported them to their destination, still unknown to Sela.

Drawing assurance from his grip, she held tight. "I... where are we going?"

"Let's enjoy the view for now. You'll see soon enough."

She had a feeling she knew where, but she kept that to herself—in case it would spoil Evan's fun.

The helicopter quickly left land and ushered them over the ocean. The beauty of the waves crashing into the rocky shore and the dark-blue hues of the Pacific rushing beneath mesmerized her.

A mere six minutes later, Sela recognized the St. George Reef Lighthouse. She glanced over at Evan and was rewarded with a smile that flooded her with warmth.

He remembered.

She'd always wanted to visit the lighthouse, and he'd turned it into a special memory for her.

For them.

Holding his gaze, she squeezed his hand. Evan squeezed back; the affection in his gaze—strong and passionate— sucked the air from her lungs. What was happening between them? Was it love? Did she have any hope of a future with him? Sela never wanted anything more.

The helicopter landed on a section of the roof near the base of the tower not much wider than the length of the deep-sea fishing boat Evan had rented a few weeks before. He assisted her from her seat and onto the makeshift helicopter pad. The blades had nearly stopped, but a gusty, cold wind pressed against her, roaring in her ears.

A woman wrapped in a jacket braved the wind and waved Sela and Evan inside. Once inside the base of the old lighthouse, the woman offered a pleasant smile and her hand to Evan. "I'm Gretchen with the St. George Reef Lighthouse Preservation Society. It's nice to meet you in person, Mr. Black."

"Please, call me Evan."

Sela hadn't noticed before, but with the way he smiled and his debonair good looks, women took notice. Gretchen wore a wedding ring, but her gaze lingered on Evan a little too long.

She finally turned her attention to Sela. "And you must be Mrs. Fox. It's so nice to meet you."

"Please, call me Sela. And thank you for giving the tour. I've wanted to see the lighthouse for years." David had known, but Evan had taken action.

"Oh? Well, you'll have plenty of time to ask questions. We usually provide tours to four to six people at a time, but your Evan wanted a private showing." Again the smile and a gaze at Evan that let him know of her interest.

Sela had never been a jealous woman and didn't plan to start now. Still, she wanted to remind the woman that she'd just called him "your Evan." Was he really hers? As if in reply, Evan slipped his arm around her waist and tugged her to him. She leaned into him, letting the woman know that he was indeed hers and hating herself for the knee-jerk reaction.

"Shall we begin?" Gretchen began her spiel by placing her hands behind her back and thrusting her chin out just so. "This lighthouse was constructed after the wreck of the *Brother Jonathan*, which carried a shipment of gold and two hundred forty-four passengers. Nineteen survived, and so the *Brother Jonathan* was the worst shipwreck on the Pacific at the time. And the lighthouse, once construction was completed, was the most expensive lighthouse ever built."

Gretchen led them through the medieval-type structure, and though Sela enjoyed hearing about the history of the lighthouse, Evan's thoughtfulness, his nearness, distracted her. She almost wished they were alone to enjoy the lighthouse and the memory without someone looking on.

At one point, Gretchen disappeared from view, though Sela could still hear her continued explanation of the lighthouse construction and preservation efforts. Sela moved to follow, but Evan pulled her back and into him. When Sela glanced up, he planted a kiss on her smiling lips.

"I love you," he whispered.

Emotion tightened her throat. "I love you, too."

Gretchen appeared again, her smile hiding a subtle frown. "I think you'll enjoy the view from this side."

But Evan had captured Sela's heart and mind, pushing the tour of the lighthouse aside.

Sela flipped on the light to David's workshop where she'd stolen a few hours here and there over the last few weeks to make the custom-ordered guitar.

She ran her hand over the sleek top, along the curved sides, feeling a sense of achievement, of pride in her craftsmanship. She'd forgotten just how good it felt to complete a guitar—though she still didn't feel that her work compared to David's. Still, she hoped the client would be pleased.

She'd contacted her customer to request additional time and explained the circumstances. Thank goodness none of the guitars had been touched in the break-in. It was as if the instruments had hung invisible on the wall, and only the things that could easily be replaced were tampered with, some even destroyed. And those items she would take her time replacing—the love seat and bookshelf had belonged to David's mother and had remained after her death like most of the furnishings in the house.

When they had married, Sela simply moved in with David and lived in the same house with his mother until she'd died shortly afterward. Sela and David had only been married three years when she'd died.

But even since David's death, she'd never felt comfortable redecorating. At least, until now. The burglars had done her a favor in a way. She'd taken the first step by getting rid of the old redwood desk, which now belonged to Evan. And now, she felt at liberty to keep going, except…really…she might be ready to give the whole house up. The property that belonged to David's mother then David and now Sela.

Two weeks had slipped by since the break-in. Looking back, the idea that someone had broken in seemed surreal. A dream.

But not any more a dream than her growing relationship with Evan. When she considered the events that had transpired these last few weeks, she struggled to wrap her mind around how much her life had changed, and continued to change.

Her quiet prayers during her early morning jaunts through the redwoods slipped into her thoughts. How many times had she cried out for God to help her to let go of David? To free her from the past, from her self-imposed prison? It would seem He was doing just that but in a strange fashion. Still, she wouldn't put it past the Almighty to be more than creative in His answer.

The floor creaked somewhere in the house, and Sela tensed, the burglary not far enough behind her yet, if it ever would be. Hadn't she remembered to lock the doors? Set the alarm? Still, she remained quiet, listening.

"Sela…" someone called, the familiar voice echoing through the house, down the hallway, and into the room converted into a workshop.

Sela relaxed. She went to the door, peeking down the hallway. "I'm in the workshop."

Clara appeared at the end of the hall and started toward her. "I brought you some cookies."

"Ah, you shouldn't have." Sela smiled, taking the tray of cookies as her older friend entered the room. "You're too good to me, Clara."

Clara drew in a breath and scrunched her nose at the smells of cut wood, shavings, glue, and lacquer. Sela loved the odors.

Then Clara smiled at Sela and squeezed her arm. "You know you're like a granddaughter to me."

After sampling a bite of Clara's amazing chocolate-chunk cookies, Sela smiled and licked a morsel of melted chocolate from her thumb. "Besides bringing me these—which we should offer in the store, by the way—what brings you out this late?"

"Piffle-wiffin. It's only nine o'clock. I made too many and thought you might like some."

Sela laughed. A widow herself, Clara could have retired but chose to keep working at the gift shop. Sela often considered inviting Clara to come live with her and had even made the offer, but her friend declined, stating she didn't want to stand in the way of Sela finding a husband—as if that were Sela's sole goal in life.

Sela thought her excuse weak, since her presence would hardly make a difference in Sela's love life. She decided that Clara liked living in the home she'd shared with her husband before he died, surrounded by their memories. Everyone was different.

And Sela had done the same for a while. But now this house, the memories, and even the furnishings, she realized, were beginning to weigh on her.

"I apologize if I startled you. I saw the lights on but got no answer at the door, which worried me." Clara shrugged and held up a key. "I hope you don't mind that I used the key you gave me."

Sela took time off to visit her sisters once in a while, especially when they went into labor. She wanted to be there to welcome her new niece or nephew into the world. Having Clara to check in on things, water her houseplants, was nice.

"Of course I don't mind, and you'll probably need that key again in the coming months, when Alexa has her next baby." Sela smiled at the thought—would she get a nephew this time? So far, she only had nieces. For their second child, Alexa and Graeme were waiting until the baby was born to learn if they were having a boy or girl. That way it would be a surprise, Alexa had said. To Sela's way of thinking, it was a surprise no matter when you learned. Waiting to hear what the baby would be drove her crazy. She wanted to start buying gifts now.

Clara strolled over to the guitar that Sela had completed. "And she's doing all right in the pregnancy? I know you were concerned."

"Yes, she's young and healthy. But even then, pregnancy takes a toll. I think she was just tired when they visited."

Looking at the guitar, Sela remembered that when David worked to create a guitar, he would refer to it as "his baby." A pang of regret nipped at her heart, and she blinked back the sudden moisture in her eyes. Camille and Alexa were both younger than Sela. She'd been married before either of them, and yet they both had children and a husband who loved them.

A family.

They both were talented women, excelling in their chosen fields. And what did Sela have that was her own?

"I don't think David could have done better on this guitar. It's a masterpiece. You're very talented, Sela. Just like your sisters."

Had Clara read her mind?

But custom-made guitars had been David's interest, not Sela's, yet she'd taken it on as her own. "Thanks, but I can't play. Not like David…or his brother, either." She smiled, remembering when he'd played again for her a few nights ago. Sela shut her eyes, allowing the melody in her mind to soothe her troubled thoughts.

Maybe she would make a guitar, just for him—an instrument created to complement his playing style and technique. Sometimes customers weren't happy with their guitars, claiming there was too much bass or some other feature of the guitar that contrasted their style. But most often David's custom-made guitars, created to match a customer's style of music, left them ecstatic—there was nothing like coupling a guitar especially handcrafted to match the musician.

If she made Evan a guitar, it would be her last, and then she could let go of another piece of her life with David.

Like the painting Evan had bought of sun rays in a mist-laden forest, sunbeams were beginning to break through the mist in her mind, lighting the way for her. Though the realization dawned little by little, she was starting to firmly believe that she'd held on to the old life she'd had with David, as well as this house, the land, far too long.

It's time to let go.

"I didn't realize Evan played." Clara arched a brow.

"You and Evan have grown close, it seems. I'm glad for you, Sela. This is a good thing. I've been worried for the longest time that you wouldn't move on."

Sela smiled, recalling Clara's words the first time Evan had entered the store. "What would you think about me moving on in a much bigger way? Say, selling this house, this property."

She'd been hard pressed to think the words, much less say them. But now that she had, the very idea, the freedom that came with it, lightened her spirits. Her shoulders seemed to nudge a little higher, and she stood a little taller.

Clara's eyes grew wide. "That would mean giving up your store, too, I imagine, depending on the buyer. What would you do?"

Sela heard the caution in Clara's words.

Oh, poor Clara. Sela hadn't taken Clara's job into consideration. Still, the woman had means and only worked to keep busy, or so she'd assured Sela many times. "What would I do?" *Make a family...* "I—"

"Make sure you think on a decision like that long and hard. Allowing a man into your life is one thing, but giving everything up on a whim is another."

"A whim?"

"I'm sorry, dear, that might have been the wrong word. Just make sure if you decide to sell that it's what you want, not an idea that Evan Black planted and is now watering."

Her back to Clara now, Sela focused her attention on the guitar, not wanting Clara to see how her comment affected her. Sela was a grown woman very much capable of making her own decisions, thank you very much. Somehow she'd given the impression that she could be easily swayed, and that disturbed her. "Thanks for your advice, Clara, and for the cookies."

Behind her, Clara released a long, disheartened sigh.

"I'm sorry. That was out of line. I just don't want you to do anything you'll regret. I'm afraid you'll get hurt."

"You're the one who encouraged me to love again. And now you don't want me to get hurt? You can't have one without risking the other."

With that, Clara laughed softly. "You've always been wise beyond your years, Sela. I don't know why I was so worried."

"Because you wouldn't know what to do with yourself if you didn't have something to worry about, that's why," Sela teased.

After another soft laugh, Clara said her good-byes. Sela reflected on their conversation.

Move on.

Sell the property.

Make one last guitar—a gift for Evan. Was she putting too much of her future, her new hopes and dreams, on him?

She'd tried to talk to him about her property on occasion, but he refused to discuss it with her. He didn't want her to think he was manipulating her, he'd said. But her acreage stood between Evan and his father, and in the end, between Evan and Sela.

Chapter 12

Evan stepped into his father's office. The man wasn't back yet?

He'd asked that Evan meet him in his office in half an hour. Evan decided to wait and tossed the file he carried onto his father's desk then made his way to the panoramic window to watch the whitecaps on a rough ocean landscape.

His thoughts turned to the day he and Sela had gone deep-sea fishing with Tom. He glanced at the pier in the distance but saw no one there. The waters had been calm that day, and it marked the first day he'd spent in Sela's company on a friendly date. The first time he'd met her, he'd known she was special, and now he knew she was priceless.

A treasure that meant everything to him. A treasure he feared would be lost forever when the ship he was on, captained by his father, crashed against the rocks and sank.

For a long list of reasons, he was terrified he'd lose her. His father, not at the bottom.

He scratched his head and sat down to wait. Not a day went by that he didn't worry his father would bring up the property again. But he hadn't. Nor had he said anything to Evan about losing his chance at that promotion.

Evan slumped down in the chair and squeezed the bridge of his nose. More than anything, he hoped the incident was behind them. He didn't like seeing that side of his father. So he'd shoved that image away, yet remained cautious—diligent to protect Sela's interests.

Michelle stuck her head through the crack in the door. "Evan, your father will be another fifteen minutes, and you have a phone call—Mr. Sherman on line two."

"Thanks. I'll take it in here." Evan stood and walked around to the other side of his father's desk to more easily reach the phone. He answered the call and spent three minutes listening to Sherman's concerns over some of the specs Evan had sent him on the houses they planned to build.

Ending the call with promises of a resolution, Evan felt tired and drained. He glanced down and saw a new sketch of the Smith River project complete with golf course, privacy fence, and gate. Something was a little off about it. He glanced at the wall where his father had hung a larger copy of his original vision.

Evan frowned, realizing what had changed. If he hadn't been so tired, he would have spotted the problem right off. Sela's three hundred acres had been included in the new drawing. Blood roaring in his ears, Evan clenched his fists.

His father stepped into his office—perfect timing as usual. "Sorry I'm late." Then he stopped in his tracks.

Evan held up the sketch. "When were you going to tell me about this?"

Robert Black found his composure and strode confidently to his desk, obviously expecting Evan to get out of his chair. Evan rose but didn't move.

"I don't know what you mean. You've known about this plan all along. Kudos to you for the work you're doing with Sela."

The room, his father's face and suit turned blood red. "My seeing her has nothing whatsoever to do with her property. In fact, I've refused to discuss it with her. She can make her own decision without coercion from me."

A nerve ticked in his father's cheek.

"For the last time, you need to tell me what's going on," Evan said.

"I think it's perfectly clear. The entire development is being held back by three hundred acres. Imagine the value of this project if the Smith River runs through it. It's just three hundred acres, and I'm prepared to offer her top dollar."

Evan felt as if his lungs had deflated. "Just give it up, will you? For me…" This woman was important to him. But his father was important to him, too.

"Tell you what, Evan…" His father strolled around his desk and to the window, like he did when he was about to say something profound or negotiate. Evan feared the latter. "You have good looks, money, and power. You can have any woman you want. You want Sela Fox, fine. Live anywhere you want. Just not in that little house on the Smith River."

Evan finally moved to stand next to his father, preparing to deliver his own words. But the elder Black continued:

"You get me that property, and then you can take your Sela wherever you want to go. Marry her, take her on a long honeymoon—my treat—and build her a house somewhere she'll be happy. You'll be able to do it all in style because you are a vice president in this company and my right-hand man. This will be your company one day. You helped to build it, and you're my son. I made a mistake in how I've approached this potential acquisition, and I apologize for my lack of tact. Do we have a deal?"

Evan swallowed the knot that dared to grow in his throat now. How he wished he could do just that, take her away from here. Just the two of them. But if she sold her property just to make Evan happy, he would feel like he'd been used by his father, and every foul thing he'd thought about the man recently would be true. He would feel that one way or another his father had won—because Evan had met Sela, fell for her, and in the end, she sold her property for reasons not her own.

His father eyed him. "I can see you're thinking about it. Take your time but not too much longer. Time is running out."

"Excuse me, Evan, Mr. Black…." The familiar feminine voice washed a surprise-filled thrill over Evan. He turned to see Sela, standing there wrapped in a white fleece sweater and pale blue jeans.

"Sela." He smiled, glad to see her and yet…not. "What are you doing here?"

"May I come in?" She directed the question to his father as much as to Evan.

"Please, have a seat," his father said. "Evan and I were just talking about you."

Evan tossed a daggered glimpse at his father, who appeared to ignore it.

Pink colored her cheeks. "Really? Maybe that explains the sour look on your faces."

"Dad was kidding. We weren't talking about you." *We were talking about your land. Mostly.*

She studied Evan for a second, searching his gaze. For

what, he didn't know. All he wanted to do was get out of here with her. Leave his father to his own insanity because it was driving Evan crazy, too.

Sela drew in a breath then glanced at her hands in her lap. "I'll get to the point. I'm selling my property to you, Mr. Black."

"What?" Evan stepped forward, recoiling at the vehemence in his words. "No, you're not." Fueled by frustration, by what almost felt like betrayal on Sela's part, Evan faced his father. "She is not selling, especially not to you."

Sela suddenly stood, her face awash with hurt, fire in her eyes. "Thank you for your vote of confidence, Evan." She turned and rushed from the office.

Evan glared at his father as he headed to the door. In return, his father smiled and shrugged. "I believe the lady has made up her own mind, just like you wanted."

Hurrying out the door, Evan jogged down the hall and found Sela taking the stairs instead of the slow-as-molasses elevator. "Sela, wait," he called. She kept moving.

Finally he stood in her path. "Sela, please, I'm sorry." He ran his hand down his face. "This whole thing is making me crazy."

"I see that," she said, a belligerent frown still in place.

"It's your decision. I know that, but why didn't you talk to me about it first?"

"I tried several times. But you didn't want to talk about it, remember?"

"And you know why. I don't want my father's plans, the reason for my meeting you in the first place, to come between us. I don't want you to ever blame or resent me if you one day regret selling."

"And I don't want the land standing between us anymore. Or standing between you and your father. I thought… I thought you'd be happy that I wanted to sell."

"Look…can we talk about this tonight?" Evan's pulse stammered as he waited for her reaction.

Please, God, let her wait until we can discuss it.

She hesitated but finally offered a subtle nod.

Evan's pulse calmed, his relief palpable. At least she'd given him that much. "Please promise me you won't go forward with this, you won't sign anything, until we've talked. Will you trust me?"

"I want to, Evan."

Desperation lodged in his throat. "That's all I'm asking. Wait for me on this."

What was he doing? He was going to lose her and not because of his father. This was all a big mistake. He cupped Sela's face with his hands, and when she didn't resist, he pressed his lips against her forehead, the tip of her nose, and then softly against her lips. There he remained, savoring the essence that was Sela. She responded, and he sensed her desperation, her need for assurance.

The doubt that still lingered.

He thought he could change the course set by his father, but too late he realized he hadn't changed a thing. That calm waters were behind them. Treacherous seas tossed them forward, driving them toward a rocky coast.

In the same shipwreck, he was about to lose both his father and Sela, the woman he loved.

A priceless treasure that could never be recovered.

Chapter 13

What did he say to his father? How did he get the truth from the man? He wasn't sure if this was the right time, considering how angry he was. Nor was he certain he wasn't overreacting, but nothing about the situation sat right with him. When he shoved the door open, his father wasn't in his office.

He turned to see Michelle ending a phone call. She frowned. "He's gone for the day, Evan. Cancelled the rest of his meetings and appointments."

"Did he say where he was going?"

She shook her head, concern ridging her brows. Evan left her to make excuses for his father's absence. What had gotten into the man? Evan had never seen him leave with a full schedule.

Stalking across the parking lot to his Tahoe, Evan tried to call his father, but the man wasn't answering his cell. Had he gone to see Sela? Evan fumed at the thought. Before he went all the way to Sela's, he drove through town, looking for his father's black Navigator at the few places he might be. Finally, he spotted the SUV parked at the Del Norte Country Club.

Not good.

That meant his father—who didn't golf—was there to take advantage of the full bar. Something had set him off. Was he finally feeling guilty about the wedge he was driving between himself and his son, between his son and the woman he loved?

All over three hundred acres of prime real estate.

Evan slid from his own SUV, closed and locked the door. It was clear his father knew how Evan felt about Sela given he'd instructed Evan to marry her, take her on a long honeymoon, and build her the house of her dreams. If the circumstances weren't so dismal, Evan might have allowed a smile. There was nothing he wanted more than to do those things—but not with this shadow hanging over them.

Heaviness pressed against his heart as he entered the club. This time of day, there weren't many patrons, and Evan quickly spotted his father sitting on a stool at the bar. Evan slid onto the seat next to him and folded his arms. He hated bars.

He keenly felt the contrast between this place and the peace he'd finally captured by spending time reading the Bible, spending time with his Father the Creator. Evan clung to that now, as he hoped to make peace with his earthly father. Maybe Sela was right—selling the land, removing the obstacle, would bring that peace.

But no. His gut soured at the thought. Sela's property—now a thorn in his side—was only part of the problem. The pain went much deeper. The issue couldn't be so easily resolved.

His father drank the contents of a shot glass, and then another, but never acknowledged his son.

Finally, Evan released a weighty sigh. "We need to talk."

When his father angled his head, his eyes were glassy and red. How much had he already had? The man could usually hold his liquor. Maybe what Evan saw in his eyes was something else.

"Can we go someplace private, Dad?"

"The time for talk is over. It's too late for that." His father's speech was just on this side of slurred. Evan couldn't believe he'd come here intending to get plastered. That wasn't like him.

"What exactly does that mean—'It's too late'? Do you know something I don't?" And *that* was one thing Evan intended to figure out. One way or another. Everything, everyone that was important to him, depended on it.

He slid from the stool and grabbed his father's arm. "Come on. I'm taking you home."

Twenty minutes later, his father sat in his recliner and stared across the living room, looking catatonic. Evan brewed strong coffee but knew there was much more going on than a few drinks too many.

The coffee ready, he fixed it the way his father liked and sat next to him, offering the cup. His father shoved it away.

"Dad, what's going on? I've never seen you like this." Fear squeezed out worry in his gut. He sent up a silent prayer to his heavenly Father, hoping for answers.

"'For there is nothing hidden that will not be disclosed, and nothing concealed that will not be known or brought out into the open.'"

The scripture drifted from somewhere deep inside— something that was beginning to happen more frequently.

"What did you mean earlier when you said it's too late to talk?" Evan took a swig of the coffee himself, sensing that he was going to need the edge caffeine would give him.

"I should never have told them about the gold, Evan."

Gold? Evan studied his father, confusion tangling his thoughts. Was his father finally losing it? "What are you talking about?"

"I owe significant money to the wrong people, Evan. I shouldn't have told them about the gold."

That didn't sound good. Not good at all. Evan huffed a laugh. "You keep saying that. You want to explain that to me, because I have no idea what you're talking about."

"How do you think Blackwood Development has kept above water these last few years, when real estate and development markets have crashed? I took out a loan and then another."

Evan couldn't believe what he was hearing, or that his father hid this from him. "You said you owe money to the wrong people. You mean the loans didn't come from a bank?"

A dark look came into his father's eyes. "They've been putting pressure on me to pay up. I thought…I thought I'd have that land by now. But you had to be noble. Self-righteous."

Standing to his feet, Evan needed to catch his breath, give his lungs room to breathe. "For the last time, what does Sela's property have to do with anything? How can three hundred acres save you from whatever you got yourself into?"

"I did this for you, Evan. Tried to save this company for you. I didn't have a choice; I had to tell them about the gold."

Through gritted teeth, Evan forced his next words. "What gold, Dad? Tell *me* about the gold now."

"Gold is hidden under the house. David's mother hid

it there. It would be more than enough to pay them back. More than enough. Worth millions."

Where did the gold come from? *The break-in...*

Evan pulled his father to his feet. "Could this have anything to do with the break-in at Sela's house?"

"I don't know." His father's eyes grew wide. "After you left to follow Sela, I received a call. I explained that I'd have the money to them soon. Because of the pressure they put on me, I told them the details. That she was selling and I'd have the gold to them soon. That it was hidden under the house. But, they told me I was out of time."

"Why didn't you tell me? Or tell her? Why didn't you call the police? She isn't safe there!"

How could her property cause such trouble between a father and a son?

Sela shook her head, looking forward to the moment Evan arrived; and yet, she dreaded seeing him. Clearly, she'd interrupted a discussion about her or her property, depending on whose version she believed.

Clara's words of caution came back to her. *"Just make sure if you decide to sell that it's what you want, not an idea that Evan Black planted and is now watering."*

Plopping on the sofa, Sela sighed. The reason she wanted to sell had everything to do with Evan. Uncertainty clouded her thoughts. At the moment, she didn't know what was going on between Evan and his father, what to think. As much as it pained her to admit it, she didn't know who to trust, either. Right now, she didn't even trust herself, especially to make a good decision.

The truth—that she still didn't trust him completely—clawed at her heart. Should Evan have to pay for the sins of his father? And yet, she held that over him, if she was honest with herself.

She needed time away to think, even if that meant closing the shop for a few days. She didn't want to burden Clara and the new girl she'd hired with too much.

Reaching for the phone on the side table, Sela called Camille, who would listen, instead of Alexa, who would tell her what to do. Alexa had softened a lot since marrying Graeme, but she was still a little bossy. Sela smiled—that was a part of Alexa that would never die. Her heart warmed at the thought of both her sisters happily married with children. Now if she could just figure out her own life.

Camille answered on the third ring. "Hey, sis."

"Did I catch you in the middle of something?" Sela asked.

"Well, I have paint all over my clothes, my hands, and face. Everywhere except where it should go."

"You're becoming quite the famous artist, you know. But if this is a bad time, I can call you back."

"Not at all. Crissy and I are finger painting," Camille said.

"She's only two years old, and you're giving her art lessons." Sela laughed.

"It's never too soon to start. So what's up? Everything going okay with your new boyfriend?"

Sela played with the little doilies on the sofa. "Well, that's sort of why I called. I'd like to stay with you a few days."

"We'd love to have you. I know how a different environment can give you a fresh perspective." Spoken like a true artist.

Camille directed her voice away from the phone. "No, honey, we don't paint the walls."

She sounds so grown-up now. "I should let you go before the whole house is painted. Will tomorrow morning be too soon?"

"Not at all. Crissy can't wait to see her Auntie Sela."

Ending the call, Sela breathed a sigh, feeling a little lighter. Leaving for a few days was the right thing to do.

Now. To tell Evan about her plans, and preferably before he came over. Admittedly, it was good to have someone besides Clara to tell that she was leaving, but she was in no frame of mind to discuss the property with him.

In her bedroom, Sela tugged her luggage from the closet and began selecting the items she would wear. Anxious to get away, she almost wished she could leave tonight. In fact, she'd call Camille back and let her know she was coming sooner. She grabbed the phone next to her bed to call her sister.

The line was dead. Sela stared at the phone and frowned. She'd have to call the phone company. Just one more thing. It was always something. She'd call her sister on her cell on her way there, or just surprise her.

The little Victorian town where Camille lived was a great place to shop, so she'd better take a good pair of walking shoes. A few old shirts for painting with Crissy, if she was even allowed that privilege. She grinned, looking forward to this trip.

She thought she heard a sound out front. Someone knocking on the door, maybe. Evan knew where she kept the key if he needed to get in. Sela's heart was torn—she wanted to see him, the man she'd come to love and adore. But facing him right now would be difficult at best.

She turned her back on the luggage to check on the noise and was almost out the door when Evan rushed into her bedroom, breathless. His demeanor scared her.

"What's going on?" Sela asked. "What are you doing in my room?"

Evan glanced around the bedroom as if searching for

something. He gripped her arms, and the look he gave her kept her frozen. "You need to leave."

Confused, Sela shook her head. "I'm glad you think so, because I plan to do just that. I'm going to stay with Camille. How did you know I was—"

The sound of glass breaking—a window shattering— somewhere in the house interrupted her. Evan grabbed her hand and pressed a finger to his lips then whispered, "We need to get out of this house."

Chapter 14

Sela stared at him, her eyes searching. Evan knew she tried to comprehend his words, but time was wasting. Someone—a dangerous someone—had broken a window to gain entrance.

Although he hadn't seen another vehicle or any indication that someone else had beat him there, he'd wanted to get Sela out of the house as soon as possible.

Sounded like they were breaking into the house from the back, so locking the door behind him hadn't made any difference. The person was probably already climbing through the window. Either Sela hadn't armed the alarm system that she'd had put in, or they had somehow disabled it.

Regardless, Evan had no intention of engaging the loan shark's henchmen, especially with Sela there. He had to get her to safety.

As soon as he'd heard the news about who his father

had gotten involved with, he'd feared for her life. Called her while heading there, but got a busy signal. Called 911 while driving before he lost his cell signal, but was put on hold. He didn't have time for that. This was an emergency—but could he even explain that?

My father made a loan to some bad men who want their money, and he told them where he'd hidden gold. I'm afraid they are going to hurt the woman who lives in the house, the woman I love. Oh, by the way, my father was drunk when he told me all this.

Sorting through that would have taken too much time, but he would have tried—had he not been put on hold.

He wasn't positive the men would look for the gold or harm Sela, but he'd had a feeling in his gut. A really *strong* feeling.

And that was playing out now.

Lord, help us!

All he wanted was to find Sela and get her out. But it was too late. They were here. With that much gold hidden somewhere on this property, her life would be worth nothing to them.

"What's going on?" She spoke a little too loud for his comfort.

"Shh. Someone is breaking into your house."

Sela tried to shove past him. "Well, stop them!"

"We can't let them see us." Evan held her in place with his grip.

She opened her mouth to protest—

"They could kill us, Sela." His words silenced her. Evan hated the fear that slipped into her gaze.

Taking her hand in his, he crept to the door, leading her, then peeked down the hallway.

Empty.

He prayed he was doing the right thing and took a step

then another, tiptoeing down the hall with Sela behind him. If they could make it out the front door and to his vehicle, maybe they could escape unscathed—though he probably couldn't say the same for his father, who wasn't even in the house. If those men didn't kill his father, then Evan would have a go…

No! How could he even think such a thing? And he hadn't meant it, even in thought. Not really. To say he felt betrayed, that he was furious with his father, was an understatement.

He'd put them all at risk with this—but especially Sela. Blood roared in Evan's ears. Voices resounded in the living room. Evan shoved Sela against the wall.

Then Sela grabbed his hand, taking the lead, and pulled him with her down another hallway. Down a flight of steps.

Evan stopped her.

"The basement," she whispered.

"We'll be trapped in the basement, that's no good."

"There's a window. We can climb out."

They continued stealthily down the stairs and into the basement. Once inside, Evan shut the door quietly. Too bad there wasn't a lock or a dead bolt.

His gaze fixed on the window then his heart sank. "Is that the window you thought we could climb out?"

"First, I want to know what's going on. Who are these people and what do they want? You obviously know something." Her face paled. "Did you know they were coming, Evan? Does this have anything to do with your father? No. I'm sorry. That's crazy. Just tell me what's going on." She searched his eyes. "Please…"

The truth would crush her. Crush *them*.

"There's no time. I'll explain everything once you're safe." Evan pushed a table under the small window, hoping that Sela could fit through. It would be a miracle if he could, but they had to try. Otherwise, there was no way they were getting out of this basement. Sooner or later the men would find them.

Evan climbed onto the table first and unlocked the window, slowly opening it as he watched for any sign of danger. He saw no one. This could be their only chance of escape.

Please, God.

He hopped down and offered his hand to Sela. "You go first."

She nodded and took his hand, allowing him to assist her onto the table. She glanced down at him, fear warring with courage in her eyes.

"Hurry," he said. "I'll try to get a cell signal and call the police."

She began working her way through the slim window, and Evan reached up, helping to support her at the same time he hoped for a signal.

"If I don't make it through the window, too, you have to leave me. You have to get to safety and call the police. My Tahoe is parked in the front next to your Suburban. I left the keys in the ignition, but that's too risky now. Just get away from here. Do you understand?"

She nodded, grunting and twisting as she edged through the window. Evan glanced at his phone and saw the bars. "I got a signal." Unbelievable. He dialed 911. The dispatcher answered.

Footsteps pounded the stairs to the basement. Evan's pulse raced. He ignored the phone, shoving Sela the rest of the way through the window. "Run!"

She scrambled out of the basement and reached down to help him. "Come on, Evan, you can make it."

"There's no time. Run now or get us both killed. I'll

hide and then follow you if I can." With those words, Sela took off.

Evan watched her disappear then slipped into the shadows behind a shelf, hiding the best he could. The door swung open.

Evan held his breath.

Sela hid behind a tree and watched the basement window. *Come on, Evan. Come on.* She focused on the window, willing him to appear. Where was he? Her pulse pounded in her head. She couldn't remember ever being this scared.

A twig snapped somewhere behind her. She held her breath, her pulse racing. She hunkered down, hiding beneath the foliage next to the tree. Searching the woods, she saw no one in the fading light.

Probably just an animal.

A few seconds slid by, and Sela relaxed a little. From her viewpoint, she could see through the basement window. The men had rushed in and looked around but then left. Were they searching for her or just making sure the house was empty? They hadn't looked very hard, which meant Evan had been able to hide.

Sela waited a little longer, unsure about the best thing to do. She didn't want to leave Evan, but she needed to call the police. His call had been interrupted when the men had come down to the basement, she was sure.

Evan's face appeared in the window, causing Sela's heart to leap. He spotted her right off—not good if she was trying to stay hidden—and motioned for her to remain there. Evan slid the window open again and began climbing through. Only…it was no use. The window was too small. Fear squeezed her chest. Quietly, he urged her to run.

But…how could she leave him?

"Call the police." His mouth formed the words, and she read his lips. Sela shook her head. She didn't want to leave him but knew she had to.

"I love you." Again she read his lips, and his unspoken words broke her heart.

"Oh Evan, I love you, too," she replied, hoping he could read her lips as well. He smiled tenderly then slipped back inside and out of sight.

Standing from where she'd hunkered, she glanced around to make sure it was safe. If she could make it to the gift shop, then she could call the police from there. Maybe. But then again, maybe that wasn't far enough away and she was fooling herself to think it would be that easy.

Her phone line was dead. Now she had a feeling she knew why. In that case, maybe they'd cut the phone line to the shop, too.

Evan had warned her not to try for his Tahoe parked in her drive but to get far away. There was no getting at the keys to her Suburban now. Still, if she could stay hidden…

Sela took a step in that direction and then froze.

A man stepped from the side of the shop into her line of vision. The way he looked at the building, searched the woods, his whole demeanor told her he was one of *them*. Whoever *they* were. Evan would tell her what he knew soon enough, that is, if she could get to a phone. Get help.

Sela slid around the tree and faced the river. Would she have to cross the bridge in order to escape? On the other hand, she could easily be spotted crossing the bridge. Maybe she could swim the river, but that was risky, too, and the water was cold. She hoped it wouldn't come to that.

Though the man disappeared from sight, Sela knew she couldn't risk going to the gift shop or going directly to the road in front of her house. In order to get help, she'd have to hike parallel to the road a ways before she would be out of their reach.

As quietly as possible, she sneaked through the woods at the side of her home, putting distance between her and danger. Between her and Evan. Her heart ached at the thought.

But Evan was counting on her to get help.

Reassured she was far enough from her house that she wouldn't be seen, Sela took off running as fast as she could while maneuvering the underbrush and trees.

Something or someone snagged her hair.

Her neck snapped back.

Pain rippled over the back of her head, bringing tears to her eyes and ripping a scream from her throat.

A hand slapped over her mouth. "Not that I care if you scream in pain. Just don't want you disturbing the neighbors."

Her legs gave out, but the man half dragged, half carried her next to him, not caring that tree bark scraped against her or underbrush scratched her face.

Oh, Evan. I'm so sorry.

The edges of her vision grew dark. Sela felt herself fading. But no! She had to be strong for Evan. For Alexa and Camille, for her nieces, and possibly her nephew, depending on what Alexa was having. For a future with the man she loved.

"Who are you? What do you want?" She forced the words through her fear-strangled throat.

"Don't worry. You tell us where we can find the gold, and you won't get hurt."

Gold? "But…I have no idea what you're talking about. You have the wrong person, the wrong house."

The house came into view about fifty yards away. The man gripped her arm so hard she thought he might rip it off. But she still had one arm free and had come to terms with her circumstances.

She wasn't going without a fight. She spotted a weapon in her path, and when the man dragged her past it, Sela grabbed the thick dead branch leaning against a tree. In a flash she swung it around and into the man's most vulnerable parts. Immediately he released her and bent over, clutching and groaning. Then he vomited. She'd hit him hard, but she didn't hang around to watch and sprinted in the opposite direction.

Another man stepped in her path. "You want your boyfriend to live?"

Evan? They had Evan? She nodded, unable to speak.

"Then you'll come with me. And I'll do what I can to keep Griggs from paying you back for that blow you just delivered."

Chapter 15

Evan had watched Sela long enough to see her disappear into the woods. It was quickly growing dark, too. By now he hoped she'd gotten away and would soon find help. Try as he might, he hadn't been able to get a signal. He didn't know how much longer he would be able to hide in the basement; sooner or later they might come back down.

But there was no way he could escape. He could still hear their footsteps above him and their muffled voices. They were having a discussion about the gold. To Evan's way of thinking, if the gold was hidden under the house as his father had said, the men would eventually end up in the basement again.

Sitting in the dark, Evan beat his head against the wall. Softly, so they wouldn't hear him, but he really wanted to pound much harder.

I should have known.

He should have seen this coming. This whole situation was all his fault.

Sela's involvement—his fault.

He should have made his father tell him the truth a long time ago, then all of this could have been avoided. But Evan had ignored the signs. He'd ignored his gut—the instincts that told him something was very wrong.

Still, how could he have known his father's insistence that Sela should sell her land to him had anything to do with a hidden treasure that dangerous men would want? The whole thing was insane.

How could you do it, Dad? Evan felt like his heart was splitting into a thousand pieces. He couldn't stand to think that his own father had done this to them. To think that his whole life, all he ever wanted was this man's approval, and now this.

Tears burned at the back of his eyes. He'd never cried in his life. But this…this was too much.

Lord, please let Sela make it to safety. I'll pay the price for her, if You'll just let me. None of this has anything to do with her. Her only mistake was to marry David.

But that was a little harsh. Had his brother known about the gold? Maybe he planned to tell his bride, too, but wasn't expecting to die the day he went deep-sea fishing.

No one ever does.

Lost in his self-recrimination, Evan almost didn't see that his dying cell phone had a bar. Quickly, he dialed 911 for what he hoped would be the last time.

The dispatcher answered, and Evan set in telling her that he was a captive in the basement, giving her the address. He started to explain about Sela getting away—

The door burst open.

Sela stepped inside, a bulky man standing behind her,

twisting her arm. Then he shoved her toward Evan, who pushed from the floor and caught her in his arms.

"I'm so sorry," she whispered in his ear.

He squeezed her, unwilling to speak through his gritted teeth. She might hear the fear and anger in his voice. But he'd called the police; they were on the way now. If he could just hold these guys off long enough for help to arrive.

Another man stepped into the basement. He was tall, clean cut, and something about the look in his eyes told Evan he was the other guy's taskmaster. "I told you that I'd keep Griggs here from hurting you, but I can't hold him off long if you don't tell us where the gold is hidden." Surprisingly, the guy had an Aussie accent.

The bulky one named Griggs had the face of a bull-dog—round and fat, with a pushed-in nose—though Evan had no doubt he was pit-bull-lethal with a high tolerance to pain. But who was this other guy?

"I already told you…." Sela looked at Griggs as if she feared her answer would stir his ire. "I don't know about any gold."

And she was right. Griggs took a step toward Sela and scowled. She backed into Evan and pressed hard, clearly and rightfully terrified of the man. "You should let me have a go at her now, Tanner. I can make her talk."

That they were using their names didn't bode well for Evan and Sela. He stepped in front of Sela. "Did it ever occur to you that she's telling the truth? That the gold was hidden long before she came to live in this house?"

Tanner pretended to consider that for a moment then cracked a grin. "No. She wouldn't sell her property because she knows about the gold."

Behind him, Sela heaved a desperate breath. "Why didn't I sell this stupid property?"

"She doesn't know anything," Evan said. "I only just learned about the gold myself, but I don't know where it is." Evan cringed inside. He'd run out of his father's house without waiting to hear anything more about the gold. He only wanted to get to Sela.

He didn't want to offer the men any more information. The less he said, the better. But on the other hand, he didn't know much more than what he'd just said, and that wasn't going to be enough for them.

The man called Tanner nodded at Griggs, who yanked Sela from behind Evan. "No!" He grasped at her, but the huge, sweaty man had a grip on her. Evan couldn't stand the terror in her eyes.

Sweat beaded around his temples. Where were the police? "I'll do anything you ask. Just let her go. She doesn't know anything, this isn't her fight."

"She won't get hurt if you tell us what you know."

Evan stared at Sela now, knowing his next words would hurt her more. "My father told me that there was gold hidden in this house that he was going to use to pay someone back. That David's mother, the previous owner, hid it somewhere. She's dead and so is David. So you see, nobody knows where it is." Evan saw the shock slide into Sela's face. "I think my father said it was under the house. That's all I know. He didn't tell me anything else—"

Another man stepped into the basement. "We have a problem. The police are pulling into the driveway."

Tanner scowled. "All right, who called them?" His gaze slid to Evan. "Search him. Find his cell and crush it." He shook his head in mock admiration. "Amazing you got a signal down here."

"What are we going to do?" Griggs asked.

He released Sela, who rubbed her arms. Tanner directed his next words to her. "If you want to see your boyfriend alive again, unharmed and unscarred, then you're going to tell the police everything is fine and it must have been a prank call. Do you understand?"

Sela glanced at Evan, who shook his head. *No, don't save me. Tell the police.*

Sela looked back to Tanner and nodded. "I understand."

Evan's spirits sagged, but he held on to the hope that she wouldn't comply with Tanner's request.

Please, God, don't let these guys get off that easy.

Tanner tugged a gun from behind his back and strolled toward Evan. His pulse ratcheted up when Tanner pressed the gun against his temple. At that moment, Evan wished he'd gone into the military, become a marine, something. Then maybe he'd know how to handle these guys.

"Keep this image in your mind when you're talking to the police."

"Easy, Griggs, we want her to be pleasant when she talks to the authorities," Tanner said.

The brute Griggs ushered her up the stairs. Panic set in. What was she supposed to do? Get them all killed by sending the sheriff or his deputy away? Or get them all killed by letting the law in?

Her knees shook, and she slipped on a step, but Griggs kept her steady, his grip on her arm painful. If she survived this, she'd have more than a few bruises to show for it, the worst ones on her heart.

David's mother hid gold in the house? Had David known? Kept it from her?

Griggs escorted her to the door and winked at her. Holding an imaginary gun at his temple, he pulled the trigger. She knew it was meant to remind her of the position Evan was in.

A knock came at the door.

Sela could barely control her breathing and wiped her hands against her pants. They would see how nervous she was. There was no way she could hide her panic.

Oh, God in heaven, why is this happening?

But to save Evan—buy them a little more time—she had to be convincing. She drew in a deep breath and focused on their walks on the beach. The knock came again. Sela knew if she didn't answer they would get suspicious. While that might be a good thing, it wouldn't be for Evan. He hadn't been able to explain the situation well enough, she guessed, or the sheriff wouldn't be knocking on the door—he'd be storming into the place.

Breathe in, breathe out. Just a walk on the beach.

She opened the door, feigning a yawn. "Oh…" She acted surprised and then concerned. "Hello, Deputy Hayward, isn't it?" It was the same deputy that had come to her aid when her house had been broken into. "Can I help you?"

"Sorry to disturb you, Mrs. Fox."

"Has something happened?" She slid her hand to her throat.

"We received a report that someone was being held against their will here in your house but that you had escaped." He frowned.

"I don't know what to say. That's…weird. As you can see, I'm right here. It must have been a prank call."

"The call came from Evan Black's phone. A man claimed to be Mr. Black. Isn't he the man who was with you when I was here to investigate the burglary?"

"Yes, he was here that day. But I can't imagine why Evan would do that. Are you sure his phone wasn't stolen?"

"Can I speak with Mr. Black?"

"I'm sorry, Deputy, he's not here." She lied with her lips, but with her eyes, she pleaded with the deputy to understand the situation.

"You do know that Mr. Black's SUV is parked in your driveway?" He arched a brow.

Panic played with her heart. The deputy was not going to read her mind. She had no choice but to do her best to get out of this. Make him go away in order to save Evan. But how?

The deputy watched her, studying her hesitation. Her breathing quickened. He would know something was wrong. Evan would lose his life. She had to think of something and quickly.

"Yes. Sorry. You caught me off guard there for a minute. I'd forgotten that Evan left his SUV for the day. He met a friend—a Tom somebody. This was a good place to meet for Tom, and then they drove Tom's car up the coast into Oregon to go fishing." She shrugged, hoping that sounded like a reasonable explanation.

"And when do you expect him back?"

What should she say? "Sometime this evening. In fact, any minute now." Sela smiled, hoping her quivering lip didn't give her away.

"Mind if I look around?"

Evan is going to die! Her heart zip-lined.

She kept her fake smile in place. "Deputy Hayward, you can't really think I'm keeping my boyfriend here against his will. That call was obviously a prank. I'm beyond tired, but"—Sela opened the door wide—"have a look if it helps you fill out your report."

The opened door served to support Sela when Deputy Hayward stepped inside her home. She'd done everything she could to send him away. Lied through her teeth—*forgive me, Lord*—but under duress and to save Evan's life.

A flashlight shined outside. Must be the deputy's partner searching around the perimeter of the house.

Sela's knees grew weaker by the second. If only Deputy

Hayward could save them. If only she could signal him, give him a message somehow, but it was too risky. She couldn't do that to Evan.

There had to be another way out. She wouldn't give up. She dropped to the sofa and rubbed her eyes.

"Okay, Mrs. Fox. You've convinced me everything is fine. I just wanted to make sure no one was holding *you* against *your* will. I don't see any evidence of that here." He grinned down at her. "We'll just be on our way now."

Sela stared at him, her mind and heart screaming for his help, and yet she didn't want him to know. How could he not have seen any evidence? How had those intruders left everything untouched? Obviously, they hadn't started digging for the gold yet, because they didn't know where it was. If she got the chance, she would ask if Tanner and his men were responsible for the earlier break-in, but honestly, that was the least of her worries right now.

"Good night, Deputy."

He partially closed the door behind him but stopped to look at Sela. "And have Mr. Black call me when he gets back. I need to speak to him about his phone." The deputy paused before adding, "Be sure to lock the door." He winked.

She had the feeling he might have been interested in her if not for Evan.

With the door closed and the deputy gone, Sela leaned forward and sobbed in her hands.

Chapter 16

"Well played." Tanner clapped in a slow, exaggerated way.

Griggs shoved Sela into Evan, again. He caught her trembling form and pressed her face into his shoulder.

She'd avoided his gaze. He figured she thought he was disappointed in her. But all he wanted to do was convey how proud he was of her courage and bravery as well as how thankful he was to still be alive—if only he could speak the words.

"Now that that's out of the way, we're free to search the house." Tanner winked. "You mates can wait in the basement and brainstorm your escape, or try to figure out where the gold is, which I promise you would be a faster way to freedom. I'll get back to you." Before he shut the door, he leaned in. "Oh, and Griggs is guarding the door, so no trying to sneak out of the house or climb through the window again. I think it's safe to say he hasn't forgotten what you did to him."

He closed the door behind him. Evan brought Sela's chin up to look in her face. "What did you do to that man?"

"I hit him in a very vulnerable place." Sela almost smiled. Almost.

Evan offered a half grin. "That's my girl." She'd fought. Hadn't given up. He hoped she wouldn't lose the fight in her. They had a long night ahead of them.

"I wish it had done more good. That I could have gotten away and found help." She stepped back, out of his hold. "I couldn't do it, Evan. I couldn't tell the deputy about the men. Not with them holding a gun to your head like that."

Evan slipped his hand around the back of her neck, weaving his fingers through her hair. She winced. He yanked his hand away. "They hurt you."

Burning heat—a rage he hadn't felt even for his father—rose in his chest. What he wouldn't do to get his hands on that Griggs.

"My head hurts a little, that's all."

Evan dialed down his anger. He didn't want to scare Sela any more than she already was. "We'll find another way out of this, don't worry." After he said the words, he realized they were meant to reassure himself as much as her.

By the look on her face, she wasn't sold. "And how are we going to do that, Evan? I already tried to escape. We have already called the police. They have come and gone. And still we are stuck in this basement with those men holding our lives in their hands. And for how much longer will they keep us alive?"

"I can't tell you how sorry I am that you're involved in this nightmare. And I can't tell you how we're going to escape, but I promise I'll do anything to make sure you're safe."

"That doesn't reassure me, Evan, as much as you'd like.

I want both of us to be safe. Do you hear me? We both need to walk out of this alive."

He drew her close enough to kiss her. In the midst of their nightmare, he wanted—no, *needed*—to savor what time he had left with her. He wasn't sure this would end the way either of them wanted.

Still, he was determined that she live. He traced his thumb along her jawline and over to her lips. "My life was empty until I met you. I thought I knew what I wanted, but once I realized how empty and lonely…"

Evan looked at her lips, wanting to kiss her, but drawing out his words instead. She needed to hear how he felt. "I started to search for more meaning. I started to pray every day and brought God into my life. I don't know why I ended up here, but I wouldn't change a thing, except maybe I'd be here alone and you'd be somewhere safe."

"Oh, Evan." Her voice trembled. "I know that God brought you into my life to heal my broken heart. To help me move on. I just can't believe that it will end here. There has to be a way out of this."

The kiss would have to wait. "Maybe if we could figure out where the gold is, but I'm not that sure they would let us go, even then."

"Tell me what you know, Evan. What did your father tell you?" Sela paced the basement.

"I was in such a hurry to get here to save you, I'm afraid I didn't learn much. He told me that he'd borrowed money from dangerous men, loan sharks. He needed to pay them back and attempted to buy your property because of the gold hidden here. Even though you offered to sell, he'd run out of time. It was then he told them about the gold, but they weren't willing to wait for him to close the deal." Evan watched Sela's reaction. "And that's when…I came straight over. I tried to call you, to warn you. If only I hadn't gotten involved in your life."

"You can't blame yourself. Whether or not we ever met or cared for each other, this would have happened. It started a long time ago. If David's mother hid it, then maybe it started long before we were even born. And now I understand her better—the reason she hid all those weapons. She was preparing for the day when someone would come for her gold."

Evan's heart raced, and his eyes locked with Sela's. At the same moment, they each began searching the room for a hidden weapon they could use against the intruders. The shelves holding canning supplies—some filled with canned fruit decades beyond expiration. A couple of tables, more cabinets and shelves. They looked in all the potential hiding places, each hoping to discover something she'd hidden.

"Nothing. She didn't hide anything, or…oh, wait." Sela pressed her hand against her forehead. "What was I thinking? It's the stress, I can't think clearly. I already discovered the weapon hidden in here."

Evan sagged at the news—they might have had a chance. "What was it?"

"A bush knife. She'd hidden it underneath a chair. I used the chair to reach to the top of that shelf one day for a planter she'd stored there. The chair broke, but I landed on my feet, unhurt. That's when I found the knife, secured underneath in a holder she'd taped there. And all this time I thought she was just crazy."

"I doubt she could have escaped this gang with only a bush knife." Evan shook his head, tired of feeling so helpless. "Do you think David knew about the gold?"

Sela turned her back on him, and he gave her the space.

To think that her husband had kept such a thing from her had to be hard.

She shook her head then turned to face him again. "Where did the gold come from, Evan? It's not like people carry gold around with them. Are we talking coins? Gold bars? What? Pirate treasure? Or from the gold rush?"

"I wish I could have found out more from my father. I don't have the answers."

"The only thing David ever said to me about anything valuable was that I was his treasure. And the only other worldly treasure he had was one of his prized guitars."

Treasure? A prized guitar? Evan locked eyes with Sela's once again, but he was almost afraid to hope. "Are you thinking...?"

Evan opened the door, and Griggs suddenly filled the doorjamb and then some, looking as if he'd give anything for Evan to challenge him. "Going somewhere?"

"We have an idea about where to find the gold," Evan said.

Griggs crossed his arms and arched a brow.

"This isn't some trick so we can try to escape. Are you going to tell Tanner or not?"

Sela wished Evan wouldn't taunt the man.

Griggs nodded and motioned for her and Evan to go ahead of him up the stairs. Evan allowed her in front of him, thank goodness. She shuddered to think of what Griggs would do to her if they were left alone or if he was given permission to have his way. Part of her wished she hadn't hit him, but she'd needed to try.

When Sela stepped onto the main floor, her stomach caved in. Walls had been ripped out. Pictures tossed and holes made where they'd once hung on the walls. Even the floor was being pulled up. It was the break-in all over again—but much worse. A few of David's guitars were strewn about, like worthless plastic toys. Broken far more easily, too.

The shades on all the windows were drawn, so no one, especially Deputy Hayward, could see a thing. Nothing out of the ordinary.

Tanner came out of the kitchen, and his eyes brightened when he saw her. He held one of her favorite mugs in his hands, steam rising from the top. She pursed her lips, wanting so badly to give him a few words. How dare he make himself at home while his men—and now she saw three more besides Griggs and Tanner—trashed it.

He grinned and winked. Why did he bother with the charm? "Have you two thought of where the gold might be hidden?"

Evan stepped forward, but Sela squeezed his arm, wanting to be the one to speak. So she did. "Maybe. We can't know for sure."

"Well, speak up."

"I want your assurance that you will let us go in exchange for information leading to the gold."

"And you have it. Once we have the gold and we're long gone, you're free. No harm will come to you." The man set the mug on the counter.

"How do we know you're telling the truth?" Evan challenged. "You could simply kill us after you find the gold. We've seen your faces." *And have heard your names.*

The man walked forward and held up his palms. "Mr. Black, you watch too much television. That might be true for some, but we're not murderers. I don't like to hurt anyone if I don't have to. Isn't that right, Griggs?"

Griggs grunted, clearly not in agreement one hundred percent.

"You see, Griggs here plays a little differently, but he's

working for me now, and he plays by *my* rules." The look Tanner gave Griggs said a lot. The man really didn't want them dead, but Griggs had different ideas. "The point is, keep me happy, and I'll keep Griggs on a tight leash. Now, what can you tell me?"

Evan nodded for Sela to go ahead. She drew in a breath. "I don't know if it's anything, but David once told me he had a prized treasure that he kept. It's his most valuable guitar."

Surprise registered on Tanner's face—obviously he hadn't expected that, but his expression quickly grew serious. "A guitar."

"I think, I hope, that maybe he hid information in the guitar about the gold. It's all I have."

"All right. Show me this guitar."

"I just hope your men haven't already destroyed it. David's workshop is just this way," Sela said.

She led Tanner and Griggs down another hallway, and then she entered the workshop followed by Evan and the bad guys. She saw quickly enough they'd already searched the room where David had made guitars, where Sela still did, but hadn't torn up anything in there. She breathed a little easier. Thank goodness the men hadn't started damaging the walls in this room.

There was the broken window, though. That must have been where they came in—at the back of the house where they thought they'd be undetected, but the window had rebelled and shattered on the floor.

If anything, Sela was glad for that. The sound had given Evan warning the men were already in the house and allowed her and Evan an opportunity to hide. In the end, she wasn't sure what good that had done them.

"I saved this room for last, hoping we wouldn't have to destroy anything. You see, I have an appreciation for beautiful things." Tanner looked from the guitars to Sela, his eyes caressing her face.

Evan stepped a little closer to her. Sela held her breath, praying Tanner wouldn't take Evan's protectiveness as a direct challenge and insist on dealing with it now.

He stared Evan down then appeared to reconsider and chuckled. After all, he had gold to find.

"Which guitar is it? Ah…wait. Let me guess." Tanner appeared to enjoy taunting them. He obviously enjoyed the game.

He sauntered around the room's perimeter, scrutinizing each of the guitars still remaining. Some David had made early on and weren't of the same quality as his later works. But there was only one guitar that David treasured.

Finally, Tanner selected a guitar—mahogany with a Sitka spruce top and abalone fret indicators—and took it from the hook.

"This." He looked to Sela for confirmation.

"Nice try." She shook her head. "That guitar is exquisite, yes. But that's not the one David valued."

She moved from Evan's side to a guitar that Tanner had passed on his stroll around the room and lifted it from the hook on the wall. One glance to Evan and he was at her side. "This is the one David loved." A Koa Grand concert with an Englemann spruce top. "He loved the bright fingering style and rich bass. I think you would love this one, too, Evan. You both have similar playing styles."

Tanner reached for the guitar, but Sela held it out of his reach. "Let me look first. There could be some fine detail—a symbol that I would recognize or notice that could tell us more. If you destroy it we could lose the clue."

At first, he hesitated. "Have a go at it then."

Sela angled the guitar this way and that. *Come on, David. Please show me where the gold is.* If he'd even known—that he'd treasured this guitar for more than its beauty and sound was a long shot at best.

She peered inside the sound hole as best she could but saw nothing. Her panic rose and so did her chest, more rapidly with each breath.

David didn't know about the gold. Her shoulders sagged. She'd hoped this was the answer—the key to finding the gold and getting these men out of her house and life. But there wasn't any clue or symbol in the guitar's design. Still, she'd keep searching because if she stopped…

What would Tanner do?

He answered by grabbing the guitar. Sela pressed her hands against her mouth, hoping he wouldn't destroy it.

"I appreciate beauty, but not when it tries my patience," he said and lifted the guitar, preparing to smash it.

"No!" Evan and Sela protested together, as if the guitar—David's treasure—brought them closer to him. To watch Tanner destroy it was too much for either of them.

Then Tanner grinned, pleased with their reaction and slammed the guitar against the table, splintering the wood, separating the neck from the body.

Oh, David. A sob escaped Sela.

And a piece of paper, lodged between the top wood and the main body of the guitar, slipped out, floating like a feather to the floor.

Sela gasped. *He knew.*

David had known about the gold and never told her.

Chapter 17

Tanner watched the small note drift to the floor, as they all did. The grin he'd had when he'd smashed the guitar spread into a full-blown smile. "Well done, you two. I knew you had it in you to find the gold, whether you knew about it or not."

He bent over, grabbed the folded paper, and opened it to read. His men gathered around to see. Only Griggs remained outside the circle of those wanting to know where the gold had been hidden decades before, and he kept his eyes on Sela and Evan, as if watching them in case they tried to escape. The look in his eyes told Evan that their time was short. Griggs was counting the hours, maybe even minutes, already planning his torture and their eventual death—unless Tanner kept his word.

"Looks like you men have some work to do," Tanner said. "Get the shovels, boys. We're digging up treasure tonight."

They hooted victory shouts and disappeared. All except Griggs, who kept his attention on Sela. Evan wished that man would find something besides her to interest him. Like look for a shovel. Would they search for shovels in the storage building outside? Or had they brought their own?

Still examining the hand-drawn treasure map, Tanner glanced at Sela and Evan. "This house was originally built at the turn of the century, but there have been some new additions in the last thirty to forty years. Only one of those new additions wasn't built on a concrete slab and for good reason. Whoever buried the gold there planned to retrieve it one day. Too bad for them."

He directed his next words to Griggs. "Start pulling up the floor so we can dig as soon as they return with the shovels." Tanner looked at Evan and Sela again. "We parked a ways down the road, near the river so it looks like we're fishing or otherwise occupied. We came prepared should there actually be something to dig. And we're prepared to cart something of significant size away, too."

"Bring 'em, Griggs." Tanner folded the map and stuck it in his pocket then led them from David's guitar workshop.

Evan followed Tanner, tugging Sela behind him. Griggs brought up the back as they entered the main part of the house. Their time was running out, and Evan needed to talk to Sela without Griggs overhearing him.

That David had hidden the location of the gold in a guitar, had known where the gold was and never told his wife, had to hurt. But if they could escape, then he and Sela could sort through the details—and all their confusing emotions—later.

Tanner led them to the solarium, and he stomped on the floor. It sounded hollow like a pier and beam house.

"Get to work, Griggs. Let's have that wood floor up before the others get back with shovels."

Griggs scowled, clearly not happy with the turn of events. "What about him? Why don't you make *him* work?"

Pulling out his gun again, Tanner examined it. He struck Evan as odd—violent one minute then acting like he wasn't a brutal man the next. Evan just didn't want to see him use the gun. "Maybe I'll put him to work, or maybe I won't. But it's not for you to say. Okay, mate?"

Griggs was twice the size of Tanner, but his fear of the man was obvious. Watching Tanner with the handgun, Griggs nodded, slowly.

Tanner laughed like it was all a joke. "Relax, Griggs. I'll put him to work soon enough. Go find some tools you can use to pull up this floor. The night is getting away from us, and I have somewhere to be tomorrow." He yawned as if bored.

Unbelievable.

In the movies the main character usually ended up fighting the bad guy at the end. Evan couldn't decide which one of these men he'd prefer to have that last battle with—Tanner or Griggs. But he imagined what it would feel like to release all his pent-up anger.

A noise drew his attention to the door. To Evan's horror, his father stumbled into the room.

Evan's pulse ratcheted up. The sight of his father was a punch to Evan's stomach. Tanner, Griggs, or his father—he'd take them all at the same time if given the chance.

But his father hadn't come on his own. He appeared bruised and beaten. Someone shoved him farther into the room from behind.

"Dad," Evan huffed out, then his legs went numb.

His father stumbled forward, his eyes unreadable. While his father wasn't here with them, being held captive, Evan could direct some of his anger at the man. But his father was now a victim, too—a victim of his own greed, which had landed them all in this predicament. Evan wanted to feel sorry for the man, but he couldn't. He hated the thought. He hated that he couldn't trust his own father. One glance at Sela and the look in her eyes told him she didn't trust the man, either.

"Were you holding out hope that Daddy would save the day?" Tanner asked. "That he'd called the police? I knew he hadn't because we were holding him, same as we were holding you. Waiting to see who would give us the information we wanted first. Now that Daddy's here, too, you guys can start to dig once we get the floor up and the shovels arrive."

Griggs looked up from the floor where he worked to tug boards away. "What about her?"

"What's with you tonight, Griggs? You saying you want her to dig, too?"

"No, that's not what I'm asking."

"Ah." Tanner's gaze roamed over Sela in an appreciative way—as one would admire an exquisite piece of art—but thankfully not in a lustful way. Not like Griggs.

Still, Evan took a step forward, wanting to protect her. "You'll have to go through me first."

"Evan, no." Sela tugged him back. "No."

Tanner grinned. "That could make for some entertainment. We'll need to celebrate once we get that gold. Going through you to get to her? That's a real nice idea. But it'll have to wait. Work first. Play later."

"You said you'd let us go."

"When we find the gold. I don't see any gold yet, do you? Until then, all bets are off."

Evan's heart sank. He pressed his back against the wall and slid to the floor, Sela with him, waiting for the shovels. Waiting for whatever was to come.

But he'd had his fill of waiting. He was about to act and soon.

His father finally sat next to him, but Evan had no words for the man. Would his father have anything to say to him? An apology might be a good start. But Evan didn't have time to worry about that now. He focused on the men holding them captive; his thoughts about how to escape kicking into high gear.

Griggs worked hard to please his boss. Though Tanner held the gun, his mind was clearly occupied. Evan used the distractions to his advantage and leaned a little closer to Sela.

"As soon as they find that gold our lives are forfeit," he whispered.

She nodded.

"Did you mean it when you said you loved me?" he asked.

Sela turned her face to him, her eyes tired and defeated. "Yes."

"Good. I need you to show me that you love me. I'm going to give you a chance to get away. You'll know when it happens. You need to run and hide in the forest until it's all over."

She shook her head vehemently. "No, I tried that, remember?"

"Think, Sela. These are your woods. You know your way around in the mist and in the dark. Find a place and hide."

"No, Evan, no…I'm not leaving you behind." Sela had spoken too loudly.

Tanner strolled across the room, toying with his weapon like he wasn't sure he wanted to use it but would if he had to. "No, Evan, what? What are you talking about? Making plans to escape?"

Incredulously arrogant, the man played with them. Taunted them. He didn't like to do the dirty work. He had Griggs for that.

"No," she whispered, a sob cracking her voice.

Two of Tanner's men stomped into the solarium with shovels and other tools, bags, and chests, drawing his attention away from Evan and Sela. Evan guessed they were expecting to strike it rich tonight. The anticipation of finding the gold distracted Tanner and his men, made them overconfident. Evan would make sure to use that. That was all he had left.

He risked losing everything he ever loved tonight, thanks to his father's greediness. But he couldn't blame the man alone. Evan had been greedy, too. Believing his success came in being at the top of his father's company. Earning money. Gaining the approval of his father, a powerful man. And now because he'd looked the other way when it came to his suspicions, they could all die.

Sela was the innocent victim among them. He wouldn't allow her to suffer. He would make a disturbance and hope his father would follow his lead so they could gain control over the situation.

If God was ever with him, Evan needed Him tonight. And he needed Him now.

Sela squeezed Evan's hand, hating that he wanted to use her love for him against her.

"Time to dig," Tanner said, directing his words at Evan. He held up a shovel and tossed it at Sela. Evan caught it just before it slammed into her.

Tanner winked at her. He'd known Evan would catch the shovel and protect her from harm.

Evan returned her squeeze and leaned closer to whisper in her ear as he stood. "Go with my plan, Sela. It's our only chance." He kissed her then stood, shovel in hand.

Oh, Lord, please help his plan work. She shut her eyes, fearing that Evan was making a huge mistake. She appreciated that he was trying to save her, to give her the gift of life. But everything in her wanted to oppose him on this.

Still, as she watched Evan dig alongside two other men, she knew she had to escape if she could. One of them had to get out of here to get help. She wouldn't allow his "disturbance" to be for nothing. If she disregarded his instructions, that's exactly what would happen, and he could end up hurt or dead. They all could.

His father said something to her, reminding her that he was still there. She'd tried to forget. Sela looked away, wondering how she would ever forgive him but knowing that Jesus would help her with that, if she'd only ask. She heard him scramble to his feet then saw him grab a shovel.

"How much more do we have to dig?" Griggs asked.

Tanner tugged the sheet from his pocket. He licked his lips. "A little deeper than a grave maybe. You should hit something soon."

Excited tension bounced through the room. Sela prepared to make her move, not knowing exactly what to expect from Evan but that it would have to be soon. The problem was Griggs kept glancing her way.

Did he sense she was about to make a run for it? She looked away and squeezed her eyes shut, hoping when she opened them Griggs would be occupied with digging again. When she finally looked up, Evan stared at her, a subtle communication in his eyes. Her eyes teared up.

No, Evan...

Evan swung the shovel, slamming it into Grigg's head. Chaos ensued, but Sela didn't look back.

She sprinted through the door before anyone could

react. Evan must have sensed Griggs's suspicions as well and taken him out first. She sprinted through the house, heading for the front door. If she could make it to Evan's SUV, maybe she could get away.

No one stopped her flight. Shots rang out somewhere in the house. Someone came through the front door, and Sela dashed around the corner, hiding, trying to find an escape while Evan bought her time. If he'd even survived and was still fighting.

Lord, please help him.

But she couldn't think about that now. She would use what he'd given her. Sela saw her chance—the guitar workshop. There was a window she could climb through in there—the broken window the men had come through to begin with at the very back of the house. She ran down that hallway, hoping the room was empty.

She found it dark but knew her way around and didn't bother turning on the lights and drawing attention. Avoiding the glass, she slid out the window and into the cool night. This time, she wouldn't risk them catching her like they did before. She'd cross the river to hide. She couldn't cross the bridge without them seeing her, but she'd use that thinking to her advantage.

Pausing to catch her breath, she peered back at the house from behind a redwood. The shades were still drawn so she couldn't see a thing, but she did see a man searching for her outside with a flashlight.

Her heart nearly broke. Had Evan been injured or killed?

No. He would survive this and so would she. She'd prove her love to him by doing just what he asked. Sela went to the bridge. If that man with the flashlight shone it this way, she'd quickly be spotted. She slid into the water and held on to the bridge underneath, using it to guide her across.

Cold water rushed against her, demanding that she release her grip on the small footbridge David had built for her years ago.

David. And he'd built a guitar, hiding a treasure map inside. Sela steadied her breathing and concentrated on holding on to the bridge, making her way across the Smith River. Finally, shivering and breathless, she climbed up the rocky shore into the grass on the other side of the river.

Darkness engulfed her. But Evan was right. She could hide in these woods. Lying on the bank, Sela rested for a few seconds.

The bridge creaked. Sela glanced up. The moonlight outlined a man's silhouette as he walked the bridge, heading across the river, shining his flashlight into the water. Into the woods ahead of him.

Searching for Sela.

Chapter 18

Unrelenting and rhythmic, a hammer pounded Evan's head, making it throb. He struggled to open his eyes. To wake up.

Where am I? He couldn't remember ever being this disoriented. He turned his head sideways. White lightning streaked across his vision.

The pain, excruciating.

He grabbed his head and squeezed his eyes shut then slowly opened them. His father lay next to him on the floor, bleeding.

Then the images slammed him, and he recalled what happened. His father had joined in the fight. In the end, he'd thrown his body in front of Evan, taking the bullet meant for him.

The next thing Evan knew, someone clubbed him from behind, and everything went black. How long had he been unconscious?

"Dad?" He pushed himself up on his elbow.

Ignoring the pain from what must be a concussion, Evan ripped off his shirt to staunch the blood flowing from his father's wound. At least he was still alive. Evan prayed he would stay that way. All his resentment toward his father seemed to fade with the thought of losing him.

The men were gone, leaving Evan and Robert Black alone in the solarium.

They must have found the gold and taken it. *Sela*...

Please, God... His heart begged his Father in heaven for Sela to find her way to safety.

Robert Black turned his face to Evan. "I'm sorry for the way things turned out. For what my actions have cost. I want you to know that I've always been proud of you"—he coughed then paused for a second before he continued—"but found it hard to say the words."

"Don't speak, Dad. Save your energy." Evan pressed hard against the wound just under his shoulder blade, watching his father's pained expression. "You can tell me all this later, when the ambulance arrives."

His father shook his head. "Nobody's coming to save us. That big fellow is sitting just outside the door, an ice pack to his head. We're not getting out of this alive."

Griggs. Evan thought he'd hit the man hard enough to knock him out for a while, if not kill him. His original impression remained—the man had a high tolerance for pain. "Did they say anything about Sela? Did she get away?"

"They were looking for her. I don't think they've found her yet, or we'd know about it."

At least Evan had that hope. He was glad he'd given her the chance to get away. "I never meant for you to take a bullet for me. Why did you do it?"

His father's face contorted, whether from physical pain or Evan's words, he couldn't be sure. "You're my son.

Why wouldn't I? Everything I've done, Evan, I've done for you…."

Evan gritted his teeth and looked away. He didn't want to get into this now. His father could die, and their last words would be an argument. He shoved down his pride. "Thank you for saving my life."

"I never wanted things to go this far, you know that, right? I just got desperate."

"I understand, Dad." And Evan did. One wrong decision had led his father down this path. That fact was scary, considering how easily it could happen to anyone. "What about the gold?"

"They dragged a box out. I guess they're counting it or packing it. Don't know."

"But where did it come from?"

"That's a story I wish I could have told you under different circumstances." He winced in pain.

Evan's heart thrummed beneath his ribs. Should he call Tanner and ask for help? Or would that just bring them more trouble?

His father gripped his arm. "It's just a flesh wound, Evan. Nothing to worry about. Besides, only the good die young." He coughed a laugh.

Oh, Lord, please keep him with me. Keep Sela safe. Get us out of this. How much more can we take?

"The gold. Now where was I? Long before you were born, before I met your mother, I was a fisherman."

A fisherman? Evan thought his father hated being on the water. But maybe that explained why.

"A poor fisherman, I might add. One day I was out on the water when I shouldn't have been—but again, I was desperate. That seems to be my life's mantra. I was deep trolling for salmon, when a storm hit and drove my small boat into the rocks. I clung to them, held on despite the crashing waves. But when the storm calmed, just under the surface I saw gold. Crates of coins and some bars."

"Don't tell me…"

His father nodded.

"The *Brother Jonathan*? You found gold from the *Brother Jonathan* shipwreck?"

"Before there was the technology to find the shipwreck and bring up the lost treasure."

"So you hid it here? Why didn't you tell the world about your discovery?"

"I didn't hide it under the house. I held on to it and did the research to find out the best way to convert it to money I could use to build my company. To build a legacy for my kids, if I ever had any. Eventually, I found a venue through which to quietly convert my discovery into hard cash. It was a small amount of gold, Evan—not the hundreds of millions of dollars' worth they discovered later in a different place, I might add. Just a *few* million." He chuckled, trying hard to infuse the situation with humor. "I thought maybe if I kept it to myself and I ever needed more, I could go back and search. But if I told everyone, then everyone would search, and I might even lose what I'd found."

"Go on. How did your gold get buried here?"

"Only half of it is buried here. David's mother took it from me along with my child whom she carried—whom I didn't know about—and just disappeared. Evan,"—his father squeezed his hand—"I searched for her for years."

"What about Mom? What about me?"

"The gold, son. It was rightfully mine. It took me a few years, but I finally found David's mother, living right here in the redwoods all this time. She'd built a house and was building a business. When I confronted her, she told me she'd buried the gold under the house for safekeeping. She dared me to try to take it from her."

"Why didn't she spend it like you spent yours?"

"Maybe she did, some of it anyway. She bought these three hundred acres and the house. But there was plenty left. Why do women do anything they do, son?" His father's question elicited a laugh then a fit of coughing. "Mostly, I think she wanted to punish me. Said I didn't care about anything or anyone but the gold. I thought she was crazy, but now I see…maybe she was right."

While trying to comprehend his father's words, Evan checked the bleeding and it appeared to be clotting, but they had to worry about infection now, among other things. He pressed his lips together and glanced out the door, wondering what was going to happen to them next.

"I left her to herself. After all, I had a growing business, and I'd found the girl of my dreams, your mother, and wanted to marry her. Fighting with another woman over gold would only end up in scandal. End up in me losing everything."

And in the end, that's what was happening anyway if they didn't come out of this with their lives.

His father's eyes glazed over a little. "I learned that Monica died, and I wanted to see David, but that's when I decided my walking into his life wouldn't be good for him." His father looked at him then. "I'm not all that bad, Evan. I do care about people. About you, David, and… Sela. It hasn't all been about the gold."

Evan nodded, though he wasn't sure his father cared that much about Sela. Still, he felt guilty for not putting a little more faith in his father. He'd distrusted him because of how things had looked, but that still didn't excuse how his father had wanted to use Evan and Sela or the mismanagement of this whole situation.

"It wasn't until after David died that I thought to buy the property from his wife. The gold that had been stolen from me was buried here. You understand, right? I worked for years to gain the permits to develop the land around those three hundred acres, thinking all the pieces would fit together nicely."

Evan nodded.

"But then, when my loans came due, I became desperate. That's when I tried to enlist your help."

And Evan's refusal, his standing in the way of Sela selling, had cost them all. "If only you had told me, Dad. Things could have turned out differently."

"Would they have? Would you have agreed to charm your way into her life if you knew the truth? Persuade her to sell?"

"We could have handled things much differently. More than that, I don't know."

Exhausted, head pounding, Evan laid back and stared at the ceiling, trying to think of a plan to escape. His father was in no condition to move, much less run, and Evan wouldn't leave without him. Just like Sela didn't want to leave him.

Sela, I hope you're okay. He'd told her to hide until it was over, but maybe she'd found a way to contact the authorities, and help would come after all. He was all out of ideas. Drained, he wasn't sure he had it in him to pray anymore, either.

He'd found a father in his heavenly Father, just like Tom had told him he would. But now, he almost felt like God had forgotten him. Left him for dead, along with everyone he loved.

On the floor, he could see under the table next to a window and noticed an odd shape. He focused his vision, trying to comprehend what he saw. *A gun?*

A gun was taped under the table. An incredulous grin

slipped into his face. He rested his head on the floor again and laughed to himself.

"You said Monica dared you to come get your gold?"

"Yeah, but I never did, and here we are. Maybe I should have, huh?"

"Monica was scared to death that you would try. She hid weapons all over the house."

Scooting a little farther under the table so he wouldn't be so obvious should one of Tanner's men, or Tanner himself, finally come back into the solarium, Evan peered up at the weapon. Was it loaded? And if so, was it in good enough condition to work right?

He envisioned David's mother preparing for the day when men would come to take her gold—namely, Robert Black. In the end, it hadn't been his father, but other, equally greedy men who cared nothing for the lives of others.

Monica would have needed an escape and planned for it well ahead of time, hiding a gun under this table years ago. Evan smiled. So God had provided an escape for him before he was even born.

That sounded familiar.

Not because of anything we have done but because of his own purpose and grace. This grace was given us in Christ Jesus before the beginning of time.

God, his heavenly Father, had known this day would come. David's mother had unknowingly planted the gun there for Evan to use one day.

The idea boggled his mind, and yet, the God he was coming to know better, the Creator—that was just so *like* Him.

Infused with faith and confidence, he reached under the

table and ripped the firearm from where it was bound then checked to make sure it was loaded properly.

"Come on, Dad. We're getting out of here."

Chapter 19

One man crossed the bridge, followed by another, holding flashlights and looking for her. She waited until they had gone deeper in the woods before she moved from her position on the bank of the river.

With their flashlights ahead of her, she watched where they tracked. These were her woods, and she knew them like she knew her own face. Like she'd known David. Like she was beginning to know Evan.

A pang rolled through her. What if something had happened to him? What if he didn't make it? Or the gunfire she'd heard had injured or killed him? The thoughts were more than her heart or mind could process, so she pushed them aside, preferring to hope for the best.

Once the men gave up on their search—and they would because they couldn't search for miles through the woods—Sela would go for help. But she didn't want a repeat of what had happened before.

This time, she'd wait.

She trekked to the edge of her property before the men had finally showed signs of turning back and swung their flashlights around. Before the light could hit her, she crawled into the bushes and hid in the dark fissure near the base of a redwood. The tree and surrounding foliage, along with her own body heat, worked together to keep her warm after her swim through the cold river. Her shivering had finally lessened.

She prayed she wouldn't be discovered. If the men had brought dogs with them, then she'd be facing another problem, and they would easily find her.

Crouching, she finally allowed herself to sit. The adrenaline from her ordeal was quickly depleting, her mind and body crashing. The bruises along her arms where Griggs had gripped her ached. Her head, where she'd been yanked by the hair, throbbed.

All of this she'd gone through for gold that had been hidden under the house where she lived. None of it had anything to do with her, yet she was still involved. Her life threatened.

Oh, David, why didn't you tell me?

She closed her eyes and calmed her breathing in case the men were closing in on her. *Let me be invisible, Lord.*

If David had shared about the hidden gold, their lives might have been different. Chances were she wouldn't have allowed the gold to remain. It wasn't about the money; for Sela, it was about being at peace.

Gold or not, she hadn't been at peace in years. Not since David's death. Not until Evan came into her life. *Oh... God...I don't know what I'll do if I lose him, too. Surely, You didn't bring him into my life just to take him away...*

Tears ached in her throat, but she couldn't afford to

cry. To sniffle. To give herself away. This time she had to get help.

Flashlights beamed through the bushes, but not directly on her. Sela pressed deeper into the crack, which wasn't noticeable on the other side of the foliage. The men wouldn't know to look. They couldn't possibly scour every inch of the forest in search of her.

Still, her chest ached from her pounding heart. Would she die from fear like a small bird? Seconds, maybe minutes, passed before the beams of light moved on. She listened to the men's boots crunch as they made their way back toward the river. Sela couldn't be sure they wouldn't be sent back to look, but she allowed herself a moment to breathe.

She shut her eyes.

The whining scream of a siren stirred her. She opened her eyes to the dim light of dawn. Realization came with daybreak. She'd fallen asleep, her body demanding what she needed without her permission.

But sirens—were they headed to her house? Was it all over? Sela broke through the foliage and met a thick morning mist. She rubbed her shoulders against the chill that met her still-damp clothes.

Oh, God, please let Evan and his father be all right. She had no energy or ability to think past repeating that prayer. But someone had survived to call the police. Shame squeezed her that she'd fallen asleep—she hadn't called for help. Even though Evan had told her to hide until it was all over, she'd never intended to follow his instructions on that. He had only cared about her safety, and not his own. Though still wary she would run into one of the men— perhaps fleeing the authorities—Sela cautiously trudged through her woods, through the thick mist.

A man stepped into her line of vision, and Sela froze, fearing the worst.

"Sela!" Evan ran to her and picked her up, swinging her in his arms. He pressed his face into her neck. "I was so worried. But you made it. You're safe."

Her heart almost burst with joy. "You're alive, Evan. I was afraid for you, but I never stopped praying or hoping."

He squeezed her tighter. Then after several moments, he finally released her and put her back on her feet. He held her at arm's length. "Yes, I made it. It's a long story, but the ambulance is taking Dad to the hospital now. He was shot"—his expression grew somber, before he continued—"taking a bullet that was meant for me."

"I'm so sorry."

"Don't worry, he's going to live." He watched her with appreciative eyes.

The tears Sela held back gushed forward. Relief, joy, and sorrow produced an onslaught, but Sela smiled through the tears at Evan. "It's over." She exhaled. "It's finally over."

"The hard part, yes. There's a lot more to sort through, and Dad could possibly face some charges himself. I don't know. But everyone is alive. The men have been arrested, except for Griggs. He escaped, but the police aren't far behind." Evan frowned and searched the woods. "He's long gone from this place, though."

Evan slipped his jacket off and wrapped it around Sela, who had started to shiver again. Then he took her hands and brought them to his lips. He cupped her face in his hands and kissed her deeply.

Thoroughly.

Like a man who'd suffered through a long drought. Love and passion poured from him, warming Sela to her toes. She didn't need his jacket anymore. If only his kisses and much more could keep her warm at night. She'd worked so hard to keep her desperate longing in check since David's passing. Sela pushed Evan away. "Evan...I...you stir things in me. It's getting harder to control."

Evan's grin was full of mischief; the sparkle in his eyes held longing. He'd always been a complete gentleman. Sela hoped he wasn't about to change that now. She wasn't sure how much more she could take.

"There's something I need to ask you. My timing is pathetic. Always has been. And I'm sorry if I'm doing this all wrong—"

"Stop apologizing. Just say it."

"Again with the impatience." He grinned, teasing, reminding her of his surprise visit to the lighthouse. "I love that about you."

She raised a brow. "Evan, please."

He drew in a breath. "All right. Here goes. From the first moment I saw you, I knew you were special. Sela, I can't imagine my life without you." He kissed her again, softly, gently this time. "I love you more than life itself. Will you be my wife?"

And he'd proven that to her. There was no doubt there. "Yes, Evan. I love you with everything in me. I can't wait to be your wife." The heat rose in Sela's face. "And as far as your timing, it's perfect. The first time I saw you was here in the forest mist. This is the perfect time and place to propose."

"What about the perfect time and place to marry?" He grinned again, and she could sense he was as eager as she was to start their life together.

"I don't need perfection, Evan. I just need you. The sooner, the better."

Evan crushed her lips with his. Though she held her passion back for now, they would be married soon enough.

* * *

Evan led Sela down the hospital corridor.

After spending a couple of hours with the authorities and giving their statements, Evan and Sela were finally released to shower and clean up. Sela would stay with Clara for the time being—until her home was no longer a crime scene.

That was going to take a while as far as Evan was concerned. They could remove the tape but never the memories. She already struggled with memories of David, and now she had to contend with the secret he'd hidden from her that nearly destroyed their lives.

Still, Evan hoped to remedy all that. Sela had given him permission to do so. He smiled and squeezed her hand, still devoid of an engagement ring. Before entering his father's room, he lifted her left hand to his lips.

"Have I thanked you lately for agreeing to make me the happiest man in the world?"

She shoved a strand of her gorgeous auburn hair behind an ear and smiled up at him shyly. "Not in at least twenty minutes."

Holding her hand up, he looked at her ring finger. "We have to do something about a ring, though. This wasn't the way I wanted things to happen."

"Stop worrying, Evan. I love you. The ring is only a symbol of our love and commitment."

"I love you," he whispered. He couldn't help himself, even though he was probably driving her crazy. "You ready?" Evan indicated the door to his father's hospital room.

Sela nodded, and Evan slowly pushed the door open and peeked inside. "Dad?"

His father glanced over, and his face brightened. "Come in."

Evan stepped into the room, Sela on his heels.

His father smiled when he saw her. "Sela, glad you're safe, too."

"I'm glad you're going to be all right." She sounded sincere, but they all knew they would have to work through forgiveness.

"I see by that big smile on your face, son, and the glow on Sela's that you asked her and she said yes."

Sela's eyes grew wide, and she smacked him on the arm. Evan feigned that it hurt. "You told your father?"

"While waiting on the ambulance I told him that when I found you I was going to propose. You don't blame me for that, do you?"

"No, but I do blame you for not telling me everything that happened. I gave my story to the sheriff, but I've yet to hear yours. How did you escape?"

"You would have been proud of him." His father's eyes shone with pride. Evan leaned against the window ledge and Sela sat in the one available chair while his father relayed the story about finding the gold from the *Brother Jonathan*. "Then Evan saw the gun under the table. Claimed that God knew he was going to need it one day."

Sela shook her head, obviously marveling at the turn of events just as he had and still was.

"Then Evan got me to my feet and out of harm's way. He rounded up all the men at gunpoint and held them, only having to fire one warning shot to make Tanner drop his gun, and then he called the police."

"I had to scramble to find your cell phone, and though the signal was weak, I got through to the police this time." Evan poured his father some water. "It took forever before they finally arrived along with the ambulance. I reminded them I had called earlier. Deputy Hayward was really sorry."

"I know. He spoke to me privately, apologizing. But I assured him that it wasn't his fault. He said I could have won an Academy Award for my performance. I knew I had to convince him to leave because your life was in danger."

"Thank you for that," Evan said.

"What about Griggs? Have they caught him yet?" Sela's eyes betrayed her worries about the man.

He didn't blame her. The man seemed intent on paying her back. "You don't ever have to go back to that house, Sela. Stay with Clara until we're married. Then we'll find our own place."

Still, Evan would breathe easier when he learned Griggs had been caught.

"And the gold? What happens to that?" Sela pressed her hand against her forehead. "I don't care about it, not really. But considering how our lives have been turned upside down, I'd like to know what happens to it."

"That, I'm afraid, will be disputed for months in the California courts," his father said. "I'm sorry for what happened. People and life are more important than gold or riches. I hope you can forgive me."

"Everyone deserves a second chance, Mr. Black. I'll give you that, especially considering that I love your son," she said and smiled at Evan.

The fact she loved both of Robert Black's sons didn't escape Evan, but he wouldn't be jealous of a dead man.

Chapter 20

Sela had wanted to marry Evan quickly without having to wait weeks and especially not months. But she also wanted her family there with her to experience the wedding, to witness her marriage vows.

Coordinating her wedding with a day and time both her sisters and their husbands could attend had pushed her wedding date out three months. Add to that, Evan's father had relinquished control of his company, giving it to Evan and stepping down to put all his energy into his legal battles—both for the gold and for his not completely above-board financial ventures with the loan sharks.

Because of his added responsibilities at Blackwood, Evan hadn't been able to spend the time with her that either of them wanted; many of those responsibilities often had him traveling. Once they shared the same home, some of their time apart would be alleviated. Filled with expectation, she smiled at the thought.

At least the delay in the wedding had given her time to plan for a beautiful, though conservative, small wedding and to create a special guitar just for Evan.

As a wedding present to Sela, Evan was preparing a "surprise" as well, though she knew what it was and had given him permission to surprise her in the details. He was building them a house—nothing extravagant or too big but a small country cottage in a more secluded part of her three hundred acres.

In the end, Evan had decided to scale back his father's vision for the Smith River development, putting several acres' distance between the boundaries of that property and Sela's property. Sela still considered whether to sell her gift shop.

A rush job at best, the small home he hoped to finish in time for their wedding would serve as a starter home. If and when they began having children, they would build in town, closer to where Evan planned to have his office and to the public schools—should they decide not to homeschool. Their country cottage would then serve as a weekend getaway.

Today was the day. By evening, she would be Mrs. Evan Black. Then she and Evan would spend the night in their new house and honeymoon in Florence, Italy. Sela had never been out of the country before. Her life had changed drastically from the moment Evan stepped through the mist to meet her, and so far, the adventure was almost surreal.

Staring in the mirror to put in the last pearl earring, her hands shook, making the task difficult. Her nerves were getting the best of her.

"You're the loveliest bride I've ever seen, dear." Clara stepped behind her, smiling at her in the mirror.

Sela hadn't heard Clara come into the small guest bedroom where she'd been living since her house had been demolished by treasure hunters. All she had to do was walk outside into the backyard where Clara's husband had built a beautiful, ornate gazebo. Pastor Jacob had agreed to conduct the ceremony in the gazebo, surrounded by nature.

Sela turned and ran her hands down the dress. "You don't think this is too much since this is my second time to get married?"

"Oh, piffle-wiffin. Alexa was right to talk you into it. The dress is perfect for you."

Turning around, she gazed into the mirror again and looked at the dress for the hundredth time. "I'm certainly not as slender as I was the first time I married," she said, a shard of insecurity over her more womanly figure creeping in.

"No one ever is," Clara said, laughing. "But you're still a beautiful bride."

The off-white chiffon, empire-style dress was sleeveless with one bare shoulder. The back laced up. "I've never seen a dress like this. I'm glad she convinced me to splurge, to live a little. By the way, where is she? And Camille, for that matter?"

"I saw them both giving instructions to their husbands about the littles. I'll go get them."

Sela adored Clara's term for children. "No, don't disturb them."

"Don't be ridiculous. This is your day. I'm sure they'll be along soon, but I'll see what's keeping them."

Before Clara made it to the door, Alexa stepped through, followed by Camille. Their faces beamed as they rushed to Sela and gushed over her dress. Camille was already wearing her elegant teal dress. And poor Alexa, she looked miserable—her pregnancy stressing the seams of her own dress.

Sela smiled and pressed her hand over Alexa's round belly. "You're not going to have the baby at my wedding, are you?"

Alexa frowned. "And steal the show? I wouldn't dream of it." She rolled her eyes and waddled over to a sofa where she lowered herself down.

Camille gave Sela a smile laced with concern. "She's had a few pangs already," she whispered.

"Clara!" Sela called a little too loudly, forgetting that Clara was still in the room.

"See if Pastor Jacob is here and ready. Let's start the wedding now."

"But you still have fifteen minutes to go." Clara followed Sela's gaze to Alexa, whose face said everything. "I'll see what I can do."

Clara hurried from the room.

"Some help over here, please?" Alexa was trying to push from the sofa.

Camille and Sela rushed to her side and assisted her up. Sela shook her head. "I'm so sorry, Alexa. Having the wedding this close to your due date really wasn't a good idea."

"It's not your fault. I'm just glad you were willing to wait for us to all be together. Now, pray this baby—whatever it's going to be—will come when it's supposed to."

"Does Graeme know?" Camille pursed her lips.

Alexa shook her head. "He would have a fit, considering he delivered Ricky. I can assure you he doesn't want a repeat."

"I wonder if you're going to be one of those women who delivers quickly every time," Camille said then frowned.

Sela guessed she realized that wasn't exactly what Alexa wanted to hear at the moment.

Clara stepped into the room. "Okay, we're ready. It's just a small wedding anyway, so we're all here. And Sela, your

Evan is one handsome man. If I were a younger woman, you might have a fight on your hands."

Had Sela just seen Clara's face turn red? "I'm glad we won't be fighting, then, Clara." Sela gave a nervous laugh. Not because of Clara, but because she was about to get married.

The room swayed.

"You okay?" Camille grabbed her arm, steadying her. "I don't need both my sisters down and out today."

"No, I'm fine. It's nerves, that's all." Sela smiled at her sisters and held her arms out. "Shall we?"

When Sela saw Evan standing at the steps of the gazebo dressed in his tuxedo, she understood why Clara had made her comment. Sela's heart raced at the sight of him, and she hoped he felt the same about her.

The wedding march toward him went by in a blur. The next thing she knew, he held her hand and together they stepped into the gazebo to face Pastor Jacob. Sela repeated the wedding vows as did Evan, but her mind could hardly wrap around the actual words as her heart soaked up the love from his eyes.

Evan placed the ring—the amazing, gorgeous ring he'd surprised her with—on her finger, and finally Pastor Jacob gave Evan permission to kiss his bride.

He leaned in close enough to kiss her but teased her instead, his musky scent wrapping around her.

The scoundrel! Sela pressed forward and kissed him instead.

Sela pulled herself free from the kiss, and Evan's grin spread wide.

"May I present to you, Mr. and Mrs. Evan Black."

Together, she and Evan faced the small gathering of smiling faces, a few clapping, except for one. Alexa bent over and groaned, gripping Graeme's shoulder so hard he grimaced in pain.

Evan's face showed his shock. Sela squeezed his hand. "Looks like we're getting a niece or a nephew before the night is over."

Graeme grabbed Alexa to guide her to their minivan. "No, Graeme. The baby. Is. Coming. Now. You're delivering this baby, too."

And Graeme passed out.

Exhausted and yet exhilarated, Sela allowed Evan to guide her up the cobblestone path he'd created leading to their new home's entrance.

The wedding reception that was to take place after the wedding had been postponed in lieu of visiting Alexa in the hospital with her new little boy, Grady. After sharing congratulations, Evan and Sela left the celebration for someplace more private.

The secluded house Evan had built for them in the redwoods.

Cedar shingles and stone accented the quaint French country cottage. "Evan, it's just…there are no words. I love it."

He smiled, pleased that she was happy. She loved seeing her man in love.

"And I love you," he said, teasing her with a half kiss.

Evan lifted her in his arms, and Sela giggled, the joy overflowing. Single-handedly, he opened the door and carried her over the threshold then set her on her feet.

Sela didn't want anything to take her attention from Evan, but she knew he would want to see her reaction to the home he built for them. She took in the spacious living area with its rock fireplace and wood floors and staircase, her breath in her throat.

"Thank you, Evan." Sela tugged him close and pressed her face near his then whispered against his grinning mouth. "And I have a gift for you, too."

He laughed, his breath fanning her lips. "Where is it?"

"Camille was supposed to hide it in the closet upstairs for me," Sela said.

"Ah, that's why she wanted the keys. She said she had a surprise for *you*," he said.

Sela took her new husband's hand and led him up the gorgeous staircase. It was difficult to appreciate the house with her new husband looking at her like that.

In the bedroom, Sela gasped at the detail. Evan had worked so hard to make her happy. She hoped he would be as pleased with her gift and slipped over to the closet. She opened the closet door, and after admiring the size, she immediately spotted her gift.

Sela tugged the guitar out of the case and stepped from the closet to see Evan sitting on the bed, impatience and longing in his eyes. But when he saw the guitar, a frown flitted across his face before he hid it with a smile.

Her heart stumbled forward. "This is my last guitar, Evan. I made it for you so that you could serenade me again."

He stood, took the guitar from her, and slid his hands over the wood, appreciation in his gaze. Then he positioned the guitar in his arms, strummed a few chords, and picked at the strings.

"It's a perfect fit for my style, Sela." In one fluid motion he set aside the guitar and drew Sela into his arms, admiration spilling from his eyes. "Just like you're a perfect fit. It's beautiful, Sela. I love it. And I love you. You're sophistication, wisdom, youth, and beauty all wrapped into one woman who fits me perfectly. What more could a man want?" His mischievous grin nearly did her in, then.

Sela knew his mind was as far from the guitar as hers was from her new house.

The next morning, Evan loaded their luggage into the back of his Tahoe. They were headed to Italy for their honeymoon, but honestly, Evan would have been happy spending their honeymoon here.

He drew in a breath of fresh woodsy air and tilted his head to hear the river flowing in the distance. Of course, Italy will be nice, too, if it means he's with Sela. He only needed to grab one more thing, then they would head to the airport.

His wife.

"Sela," he called and jogged back into the house. "Are you ready to go? We're going to be late."

Evan thrust his hands in his pockets and admired his handiwork. They would be happy in this house until they started having babies. His heart jumped at the thought.

What was keeping Sela? Something on the counter drew his attention, and he strolled over.

Sela had scrawled a message for him on a sheet of paper.

Evan, meet me at the river, Sela.

What surprise did she have for him now? Odd. But even stranger was Evan's growing sense of unease. He hurried out the back of the house and down the hill overlooking the Smith River.

"Sela!" He scanned the surrounding area but didn't see her.

Impatience and concern burned in his gut as he marched down the hill, trying to shove it all away. He didn't want to ruin their day with a bad attitude, but they were already running behind as it was.

"Sel—"

"No need to shout. She's right here." The familiar, dreaded voice snaked down Evan's back.

Griggs!

He whirled around, fear squeezing his throat. Griggs held Sela in a tight grip.

Her eyes grew wide. "Oh, Evan…"

"What do you want, Griggs? There's no more gold for you. Why did you come back?"

"Because you and I never had our chance to have it out. I missed the promised entertainment when we got the gold. A chance to go through you to get to her."

The man was insane, no doubt there.

Evan shrugged off his jacket. "All right then, let her go and take your chances with me."

"Evan, no," Sela pleaded.

"That's not how it works. When I'm done with you, then I'll have a go at her."

Those were fighting words, and Evan appreciated them—the man had just ignited his rage. "You're forgetting something. You have to actually go through me first."

Griggs threw Sela aside as Evan plowed into him. The force threw them both off balance and sent them rolling together down the hill toward the river. Somewhere Sela screamed.

Pain exploded in Evan's head, but somehow he dragged to his feet. If he didn't win, they would both die. Griggs's huge fist came at him. Evan dodged and thrust a blow to Griggs's ribs. The punch didn't faze him.

Evan's only hope would be to get him in the river and hope it washed the man away. He couldn't win in hand-to-hand combat. He threw himself into Griggs again, but they only stumbled backward. Griggs tripped on a rock and fell, Evan alongside him.

Out of nowhere, Sela straddled Griggs.

"No, Sela, stay back!" Evan thought she'd gone to call the police by now.

She dropped a huge stone into Griggs's gut and privates. "Not again," he groaned and rolled to his side then somehow managed to stand.

Sela dove into him and pushed him backward.

He fell into the river. But Sela went with him.

"No!" Evan jumped to his feet, ignoring his aching, bruised body. "Sela!"

He ran along the bank of the river, watching the current sweep her and Griggs away. Hadn't that been his plan? Had she known what he was thinking?

"What's happened here?" Deputy Hayward was behind Evan now, pacing with him.

"Sela and Griggs are in the river," Evan said. "I have to get her out. Did she call you?"

"No, I heard Griggs was in the area and thought to check in on you."

Griggs washed up on the other side and crawled out.

"Freeze, Griggs!" the deputy shouted.

The criminal started to run, but he didn't get far before other deputies surrounded him. They'd already been searching the area.

"Oh, Lord, please save her. Bring her back to me," he prayed, running alongside the river.

The current swelled and then slowed, and Evan ran ahead of Sela in the river and then jumped in. The water was calmer, and Sela swam toward him. Together they made their way to the shallow water edging the river's banks. Evan swept her dripping and exhausted body up in his arms.

He kissed her chilled lips. "This wasn't the way I wanted to start our honeymoon, or our life together, for that matter."

"Think about it. I don't have to worry about Griggs ever again. And this way, I was able to save *you*."

Evan grinned. "I think we're going to make beautiful music together, Mrs. Black."

* * * * *

REQUEST YOUR FREE BOOKS!

2 FREE CHRISTIAN NOVELS
PLUS 2
FREE
MYSTERY GIFTS

HEARTSONG
PRESENTS

HSP12

REQUEST YOUR FREE BOOKS!

2 FREE INSPIRATIONAL NOVELS
PLUS 2
FREE
MYSTERY GIFTS

Love Inspired

YES! Please send me 2 FREE Love Inspired® novels and my 2 FREE mystery gifts (gifts are worth about $10). After receiving them, if I don't wish to receive any more books, I can return the shipping statement marked "cancel." If I don't cancel, I will receive 6 brand-new novels every month and be billed just $4.49 per book in the U.S. or $4.99 per book in Canada. That's a savings of at least 22% off the cover price. It's quite a bargain! Shipping and handling is just 50¢ per book in the U.S. and 75¢ per book in Canada.* I understand that accepting the 2 free books and gifts places me under no obligation to buy anything. I can always return a shipment and cancel at any time. Even if I never buy another book, the two free books and gifts are mine to keep forever.

105/305 IDN FVW5

Name _____ (PLEASE PRINT) _____

Address _____ Apt. #

City _____ State/Prov. _____ Zip/Postal Code

Signature (if under 18, a parent or guardian must sign)

Mail to the **Reader Service:**
IN U.S.A.: P.O. Box 1867, Buffalo, NY 14240-1867
IN CANADA: P.O. Box 609, Fort Erie, Ontario L2A 5X3

**Are you a subscriber to Love Inspired books
and want to receive the larger-print edition?
Call 1-800-873-8635 or visit www.ReaderService.com.**

* Terms and prices subject to change without notice. Prices do not include applicable taxes. Sales tax applicable in N.Y. Canadian residents will be charged applicable taxes. Offer not valid in Quebec. This offer is limited to one order per household. Not valid for current subscribers to Love Inspired books. All orders subject to credit approval. Credit or debit balances in a customer's account(s) may be offset by any other outstanding balance owed by or to the customer. Please allow 4 to 6 weeks for delivery. Offer available while quantities last.

Your Privacy—The Reader Service is committed to protecting your privacy. Our Privacy Policy is available online at www.ReaderService.com or upon request from the Reader Service.

We make a portion of our mailing list available to reputable third parties that offer products we believe may interest you. If you prefer that we not exchange your name with third parties, or if you wish to clarify or modify your communication preferences, please visit us at www.ReaderService.com/consumerschoice or write to us at Reader Service Preference Service, P.O. Box 9062, Buffalo, NY 14269. Include your complete name and address.

LIDIR12